FAR FROM MERCY

DON'T MISS THESE ALEX ANDER THRILLERS!

Alex Ander writes what he enjoys reading – action thrillers packed with fistfights, gunfights, good-and-decent main characters, and heart-pounding excitement and adventure...all with clean language, no graphic sex, and an undertone of faith from a Christian worldview.

Aaron Hardy – Ex-Special Forces

The Unsanctioned Patriot

American Influence

Deadly Assignment

Patriot Assassin

The Nemesis Protocol

Necessary Means

Foreign Soil

Of Patriots and Tyrants

Act of Justice

The Last Kill

Two Minutes to War

Three Days in Rome

Dark Days of the Republic

Act of War

BIG SKY Series – Sheriff Wade Lockhart

Big Sky

Ambush

Reckoning

Jacob St. Christopher – Former FBI Hostage Rescue
Protect & Defend
Word of Honor
A Vow to the Innocent
Above & Beyond
Hard Road to Redemption

Jaxon Reigns – Ex-CIA Paramilitary Operations
To Reign Supreme
Hard Reign

Special Agent Cruz – FBI Agent
Vengeance is Mine
Defense of Innocents
Plea for Justice

Jessica Devlin – U.S. Marshal
Trust Fall
No Good Options
Let the Hunt Begin

Other Action Thrillers
Kill Order
Far From Mercy
Executive One Foxtrot

FREE Ebook
Escape & Evade
Go to AlexAnderNovelist.com

ALEX ANDER

TABLE OF CONTENTS

"Go and learn the meaning of the words,
'I desire mercy, not sacrifice.'
I did not come to call the righteous
but sinners."
~ Matthew Chapter 9; Verse 13

FAR FROM MERCY

TEN YEARS AGO
THE CARIBBEAN
NORTH OF VENEZUELA

Gripping a folding knife in her right hand, Mercy Sands yanked the knife's four-inch blade from a man's neck before watching him fall face first to the floor. Staggering, she listed leftward to lean against a wall. The rough cinderblock's cold, wet surface permeated her left shoulder and arm, sending a shiver down her spine. Dirt and grime from the basement wall mixed with her blood and sweat. She didn't care, though. Maybe the dirt would stop the bleeding. In fact, maybe she should roll her back across the wall to 'treat' the ten or twelve—or twenty or fifty—open lacerations she had there. She had lost count after the first left cross slammed into her right cheekbone.

With the back of her right hand, Mercy touched her swollen right eye, wincing at the 'electricity' the act delivered to the right half of her head. Her cheek was inflamed, too, possibly broken. That was fine. In time, everything would heal. Right now, however, she had to get out of this place and off the island. As to how she would escape from a private island in the Caribbean Sea, she didn't know. But first things first, she needed to evade her captors.

Mercy glanced over her right shoulder to spy a dead body sprawled on the dark concrete floor between two ropes suspended from eyebolts in the floor joists above. The fasteners were ten feet apart from each other, and the rope attached to the left one was still wound around the dead man's neck.

On her four o'clock, two feet away, her second torturer—the 'Southpaw' who had done his best to break her face—lay dead from knife wounds to his neck and chest.

An hour earlier, while her outstretched arms were being bound—at ten and two o'clock—with the ropes hanging from the overhead floor joists, a kneeling, naked Mercy had identified the guy, the one now wearing the rope as a necktie, as the weaker of the two men. And whenever her chance presented itself, she vowed to go to work on him.

Minutes ago, after Southpaw had left the chilly, musty, barely lit room, Mercy's divide-and-conquer chance had come. She proceeded to charm and plead with 'Necktie' for a drink of water, to loosen her restraints—even just one. "What am I going to do— overpower a big, strong man like you?" she had said to him before spitting out a string of blood, her lower-right molar bouncing off the floor ahead of her knees.

It wasn't true, though. Necktie was a short man—if he was a man at all. The acne on his face had suggested he wasn't yet out of his teens. At any rate, her charm had wooed him into slackening the left rope and giving her a bottle of water.

After taking a swig, she had held the bottle low while thanking him. When he had bent over to retrieve the refreshment, she had sprung to her feet, looped the left rope around his neck twice, and fell backwards. Using her bodyweight, her shoulder muscles feeling like they would tear at any moment, Mercy had arched her back and pulled with all the strength she could muster.

For nearly two minutes, Necktie had thrashed around before slowly succumbing to his fate.

Mercy had then cut herself free, using the folding knife she had spotted clipped to Necktie's front pocket. She had then padded barefoot across the frigid floor to stand with her back to the wall, the door to the room on her right.

Seconds later, when Southpaw entered, with the fingers of one hand pinching two soft drink bottles, while his other hand gripped a brown paper bag, she had lunged forward, thrusting the point of the knife up through the man's neck and into the back of his mouth.

Dropping everything after his prisoner's initial strike, Southpaw had then clenched his throat while she stabbed him multiple times in the chest, finally felling him with a deathblow to the back of the neck, sending him face first into the floor.

Now, bent over, her butt pressed against the wall, her

hands on her knees, Mercy took a moment to rest. But only a moment, for any second now, another hostage-taker could walk into the room. She commandeered a Beretta 92FS pistol from Southpaw's pants and looked at it. It was a little big for her smallish hands, but in single-action mode, the pad of her right index finger fell nicely on the trigger. But using the weapon, however, would surely draw in the rest of the gun-toting thugs she knew were roaming the grounds. The further she could make her way out of the compound, before having to set off a round, the better.

Mercy stood tall and arched her back. She was rewarded with a satisfying crack from somewhere lower on her backbone. Half ambling, half limping, she headed toward a pile of clothes near a wall.

After stepping into black panties and black leggings, Mercy eyed her red high heels before examining Necktie's tennis shoes and sighing. He may have been small, but he had big feet, much bigger than hers. Opting to leave behind her footwear and go barefooted, she picked up her bra and her designer lightweight sweater dress. The cuts on her back came to mind as she contemplated strapping on the bra. A quick glance at her 32-Bs told her she could forgo the support for comfort.

Raising the red sweater dress above her head, she let it glide down her body, grimacing when the prickly yarn grated across her open wounds. A tick later, with the stretchy, body-hugging garment in place, its hem settling around her thighs, Mercy claimed Necktie's pistol, another Beretta 92FS, and headed for the door.

Stopping in the doorway, she peeked out to scan left and right. The way was clear. Fortunately, having infiltrated Nestor Romero's criminal organization a year ago—as an add-on to the female entourage that sauntered around the grounds, lounged by the pool, or accompanied Romero on visits to nightclubs—the 25-year-old, five-five, long-legged and curvy undercover ICE agent knew the layout of the trafficker's Caribbean hideout. The downside of that knowledge, however, was she also knew the multitude of armed gunmen stationed between her and her way off this island.

After blowing a lock of dirty-blonde hair out of her face, hair stained with more of her blood and sweat, Mercy cut a length of shoelace from Necktie's tennis shoes, clipped the dead man's wood-handled COAST FX411 folding knife inside the waistband of her leggings, then tied her long hair into a ponytail.

With a Beretta in each hand, pointing each pistol upward, the muzzles near her temples, she closed her eyes, the swollen right one throbbing as she did so. She took a deep breath, held it, then slowly exhaled. A couple beats later, she opened her eyes, steeled herself for what was to come, then took a step forward, her mental voice saying to herself, *A lot of people are about to die.*

With her bare feet on the wooden planks of the basement steps, Mercy peeked through the gap at the bottom of the door leading to the main floor. Seeing a pair of shoes facing away from her, she used the muzzle of the Beretta 92 in her left hand to slowly push open the door while pointing the other 92 to the right as she cleared that side of the kitchen.

In Spanish, a man's voice: "¿Eres tú otra vez, Johan? — *Is that you again, Johan?*"

After glancing through the vertical crack to her left, and confirming the rest of the room was empty, Mercy laid the right 92 on the floor, sneaked up the stairs, snaked around the half-open door, and approached the seated Venezuelan, a scowl on her face as she tried to recall his name. *Angel? Adrian?*

Holding a sandwich in his hands, 'Angel-Adrian' slowly turned his upper body clockwise.

Withdrawing her right hand from under her sweater dress, Mercy thumbed open the COAST knife, stuck the drop point blade into Angel-Adrian's right ear, then drove his face forward into a bowl of thick soup to stifle any involuntary cries.

His body went limp, and his sandwich plopped onto the white tile flooring.

Mercy folded the FX411, stowed it inside her

leggings, then reclaimed the second Beretta. Bypassing her victim, while heading for the kitchen archway, she spotted a bowl of mixed fruit on a counter beside her. She plucked a few grapes from a sprig, popped them into her mouth, then advanced deeper into the home before stopping at a hallway. *Andrés*, she thought while chewing, grateful her beating hadn't damaged her memory at least. *That was his name.* Lifting her arms to point her guns straight out at nine and three o'clock, she stepped into the intersection and whipped her head back and forth.

Clear.

Rotating her arms and guns inward, she moved forward, aiming the Berettas ahead of her as she came to a wide archway, an archway that led to a cavernous living room with a ceiling two stories up. On her ten and two o'clock, staircases built into the walls took people to the second and third floors. And anyone looking down from those upper floors would easily spot her.

Outside, loud and upbeat Latin music and rowdy screams poured in through open main-floor windows, most likely coming from the backyard pool. Daytime highs had been expected to hit eighty, and the girls had been talking about an impromptu pool party. In fact, Mercy had been seconds away from trading her leggings and sweater dress for her bathing suit when two of Nestor Romero's goons had burst into her room and dragged her down to the basement.

Mercy cast a backward glance before surveying the

massive living room again. After squatting, to get as much of a look at the upper level as she could, she stood tall and planned her path around the many household items—couches, easy chairs, end tables, and floor lamps—that lay before her. She was forced to pass through this 'kill zone' if she wanted to make it off the island.

Voices came from behind her, from the hallway she had passed by earlier.

She faced the voices, glimpsed her pistols, then turned away. *Still too soon.* She could shoot them before they could get off a shot. That much she knew for sure. But she still had a long way to go and a lot of henchmen to get past.

The Latin music picked up in intensity.

Mercy squinted at a window near the backyard. The music might give her cover if she had to fire. Both inside and outside, people would first question what they had heard. *Was that a gunshot or just a loud noise? Or are my ears playing tricks on me?* Those questions would delay a gunman's reaction time, buying her a few seconds. And a few seconds might make the difference between life and death.

The oncoming voices drew closer.

Mercy marched ahead, entering the living room with her arms straight out above her head, Berettas aimed at the upper-level wooden railings. Moving swiftly, her head tilted backward, her body spinning left and right, she alternated from scanning for targets to searching for objects in her way, her 92s always pointed upward.

The voices were nearly upon her.

Two half spins and a few backward steps later, realizing she would never make it without being spotted, she squatted behind a brown leather sofa, out of sight from the approaching men; but a sitting duck if someone from above happened to look down.

The men entered the living room.

Staying low, she listened. Hearing them moving to her right, she crept to her left, always keeping the sofa between them and her.

Moments later, crouching behind the sofa's right arm, she watched them disappear down a different hallway across the room. She let out a slow, silent breath of relief.

From above: "Tú allí. ¿Qué estás haciendo? — *You there. What are you doing?*"

Hunched over, Mercy drew her guns closer to her stomach. "Nothing." She paused. "Just...just looking for a lost earring." She had no idea if he understood English. Most of Romero's men knew at least some. She stood and strolled away from the sofa with her guns hidden from him.

"Detener — *Stop*."

Mercy stopped.

"Ven aquí — *Come here*."

Mercy shut her eyes. *No. Can't do that.* She whirled left, threw her left arm out and upward, and squeezed the

Beretta's trigger three times.

Two bullets hit her inquisitor in the chest while the third hit him in the face.

He went down hard and never moved.

The few seconds of lead time she had hoped the loud music would afford her never came, as the line of questioning had caught the attention of a second man. He materialized as his colleague had been falling to the floor.

Mercy felled the second man with four rounds to his center of mass.

He jigged in place before dropping.

The two men who had just left the living room rushed back into the space with their guns drawn.

Mercy let loose with a hail of gunfire from both pistols.

The two men staggered backward then collapsed.

Gunfire from above forced Mercy to take cover at the end of a bookcase against a wall.

Incoming rounds bore holes into hardbacks and paperbacks, sending shredded paper into the air.

She leaned out, fired, then pushed her back to the wall again.

More projectiles thudded into the collection of novels on her left.

She fired back until her right Beretta ran dry. Tossing it, she transferred her remaining pistol into her right hand, dropped the gun's magazine into her left palm, and counted six rounds. *Seven left*, she said to herself.

From up above, two guns roared. Another gunman had joined the fight.

She let them get off several more shots. When a lull came, she charged away from her hiding place, firing upward while making a dash toward the two dead men across the living room. The door to the backyard was closer. But with an empty gun, she stood little chance once she exited the house.

Her fourth wild shot got lucky, and one man above took a round to the shoulder. He grabbed his right arm and yelled.

Three trigger pulls later, the slide on the Beretta locked to the rear. She let go of the gun, slid to her knees, scooped up the nearest dead man's pistol—immediately feeling comfortable with the grip—and killed both men above her with a half dozen perfectly placed shots.

The man nursing the arm injury fell backward while the other one tumbled over the railing. He crashed onto a floor lamp, breaking it in half, before knocking over an end table.

Mercy glimpsed the gun she held, a Sig Sauer P320 Carry model 9mm, the same weapon the ICE agent carried when she was on duty. *No wonder it felt so comfy.* She plucked a spare 17-round magazine from her dead benefactor's pants pocket and bolted back the way she had come.

     FAR FROM MERCY

•••

Mercy emerged into the light of a setting sun behind her. The three-story mansion, also on her six o'clock, was already blotting out the warm rays on the near side of the in-ground pool ahead of her. She fast walked across the lawn, the prickly grass feeling good, invigorating the soles of her feet.

Even though the temps had already fallen off at least ten degrees from their daytime highs, bikini-clad girls still lounged by the shaded pool. A few were even courageous enough to be splashing around in the water.

Her eyes darting left and right, searching for gunmen, Mercy padded down a smooth stone walkway.

Off to her right, she stared down a young kid in his late teens. Romero hired a lot of young kids. Whether abject poverty, or pretending you were a tough guy with a gun, had drawn them to the trafficker, she didn't know. What she did know, however, was that if you were old enough to carry a gun, then you were old enough to die. She raised her right hand out to her side and killed him with three shots to his chest while he was still fumbling to draw his pistol.

Girls screamed.

Mercy turned right and walked backwards. Seeing no one on her 'six,' she did another clockwise one-eighty and plodded forward, the shady pool water on her immediate right, a dozen lounge chairs lined up on her left, on the six-by-six-foot concrete pads that encircled the pool.

Dripping wet, the black hairs on his chest and arms plastered to his skin, a darker-skinned man in the pool gripped the stainless-steel ladder railings and stepped up from the water.

Approaching him, the ladder on her right, she recognized him as Miguel, another of Romero's men. This guy, however, had a reputation for getting his way with the women, whether they wanted it or not. Staring into the distance on her two o'clock, she put three quick shots into Miguel's face while spotting a figure cutting around a row of hedges a hundred feet away.

With a heavy splash, Miguel fell backward, his blood immediately tainting the clear liquid around him like drops of food coloring in a glass of tap water.

Gunfire from the hedges made Mercy duck behind an overturned lounge chair. It wasn't cover, but an inexperienced shooter would not have the sense to simply blast through the chair. No. An inexperienced shooter would wait for a clear sight picture.

Mercy used the delay to line up her sights and squeeze off a long shot.

Her bullet hit its mark.

The figure clutched his chest and keeled over sideways.

More gunshots came from her right, from across the width of the pool.

    FAR FROM MERCY

She spotted a gunman using fleeing women as human shields. *Coward.* Rising to a squat, she sidestepped left while firing above his head, making him duck as she waited for her opportunity.

One of his shots hit a woman in the side.

Squealing, she grabbed herself and spun into the water.

When the last woman had bypassed the shooter, Mercy took aim and sent a single round into his nose.

His head rocked backward before he fell forward into the pool beside the flailing woman he had shot.

Mercy looked back at the house and saw a half a dozen armed men storming out of the structure. She took off running, thumbing the magazine release on her P320 a split-second ahead of slamming home a fresh seventeen. She had the gun operational again before the empty mag bounced off the concrete. Veering right, she snagged a blue-and-white pool ring buoy, shouting, "Here, catch," while tossing it to the wounded girl in the water.

Gunshots.

As the buoy hit the water a foot from the girl, bullets zipped by Mercy, one shattering a bottle of beer on a poolside table before glass shards landed near her red-painted toenails.

Twirling right, she stumbled and teetered. At the last second, she put her left hand down on the concrete and saved herself from falling. Squatting, she fired a few rounds toward her pursuers, then rose up and sprinted toward the hedges. Every fourth or fifth stride, she changed course to keep her assailants from getting a bead on her.

•••

Ten feet from a gap in the hedges, a running Mercy reached out behind her and got off several shots before bolting through the gap and making a hard right, putting a visible barrier between her and her would-be killers.

A 'first down' away, a rifle-toting man saw her coming his way.

Facing forward, her eyes growing bigger, she fired her Sig.

Her pistol spewed two rounds before the slide locked to the rear.

One of her rounds went wide. The second hit him just under his left collarbone.

He howled while bringing his right hand to the injury.

Closing the distance, Mercy gripped her empty P320 by the muzzle and threw the gun at him as if she were throwing a tomahawk.

The 26-ounce pistol struck a glancing blow to the right side of his head.

He shook it off while nursing his bullet wound.

She crashed into him before he could get his slung rifle up and on target.

The two tumbled and rolled.

Mercy gained control of the rifle, a 5.56mm AR-15 variant, and tried to point it at him; however, the sling had become entangled around the man's neck. So, she trundled onto her butt and put both feet on his shoulders, her left foot pressing on his wound.

Screaming, he threw his head backward, the back of his neck hitting her pubic bone.

She arched her back and yanked on the AR-15.

Choking from the sling cutting off his airway, he fought back, thrashing around on the sandy shoreline, dragging her with him as he struggled to get away.

During the collision and subsequent tussle, Mercy's sweater dress had been wrenched up to her waist, and her leggings had been pulled down to her thighs. Now, being dragged along the beach, sharp stones and gritty sand were slipping past her underwear, intruding into places where stones and sand shouldn't go.

Unlike in the basement, though, Mercy didn't have the two minutes it would take for this guy to expire. Plus, her lady parts couldn't take much more of this sandpaper-like grinding going on. Seeing the COAST clipped to her rolled-down leggings, she coiled her left arm around the AR-15. Following another hard tug on the rifle, she leaned forward, grabbed the folding knife, thumbed it open, and jammed the point into the man's left eye.

Bellowing in pain, he diverted all his energy toward

his fresh wound.

Retracting the four-inch blade, she then drew it across his throat.

Blood spurted three feet into the air before arcing downward and staining his khaki pants.

With two quick strikes, Mercy sliced at the sling to free the AR-15 then rolled to her knees. Hoisting her leggings up to her waist—sand and all—she stood, shot the man, claimed a spare 30-round magazine from one of his vest's pockets, then raced down the beach, toward a boathouse at the start of a long wooden pier. Moored at the far end of that pier, facing away from her, a white yacht bobbed up and down against the backdrop of a blackening sky meeting darkening waters.

...

Down on one knee, the AR-15 to her left shoulder, Mercy emptied the gun in five, full-auto bursts. This AR-style rifle had been modified for full-auto and three-round-burst mode.

The six men chasing her dove for cover as the sand around their feet erupted into the air.

Backing up to the boathouse door, she reloaded the AR-15, fired a short full-auto string, then scampered into the structure while flicking the fire selector switch to three-round-burst mode.

        FAR FROM MERCY

Inside the boathouse, a white Sleekcraft speedboat, with red and gray trim, was anchored to an L-shaped dock.

Mercy stared at the Sleekcraft in front of her. *The speedboat would be faster, but,* she glimpsed the yacht a hundred feet away on her nine o'clock, *the yacht has more range.*

Perspiring, feeling her skin becoming clammy, she closed her eyes and bent over a bit. Her body was rebelling against the last hour's rough treatment. She drew in a few breaths, slowly letting out the air each time. *Keep it together, Mercy. You're almost home.*

Raising the AR-15, she backed up, leaned outside the boathouse, and touched the trigger twice.

Two three-round bursts left the barrel.

She ducked back inside and jumped into the speedboat. *That should keep them honest.* After searching a couple storage bins, she found a gray case, lifted its lid to find what she had hoped was in there, then shut it again.

Mercy leaped from the boat, opened and tipped over two gas cans in the boathouse's corner, retrieved a dirty rag, then picked up a half-full gas can. Soaking the rag in gasoline, she removed the speedboat's gas cap and shoved the material into the tank's nozzle.

After dousing the speeder with the rest of the fuel,

she ran down the dock, out of the boathouse, and down the pier.

Halfway to the yacht, she whirled around to see two of her six followers ten yards from the boathouse door. She fired two bursts then made a mad dash for the yacht.

Return fire tore chunks of wood from the pier as she hopped onto the ship. She fired two more bursts, undid the mooring lines, then hurried to the helm to start the engines.

Spinning around, Mercy emptied the AR-15 at two men running toward her. She then hauled out a flare gun and two flares from the gray case she had confiscated from the speedboat.

With the emergency gun loaded, she aimed and sent the first flare toward the approaching men on the pier.

One man jumped into the water while the other laid out flat on his belly.

Mercy reloaded the gun then fired a second flare toward the speedboat that was being boarded by the other four gunmen.

A red fireball zipped into the boathouse.

Flames erupted from the building, engulfing the speedboat as the men jumped overboard.

Two seconds later, an explosion blew the roof off the boathouse, launching building materials high into the air.

Mercy faced the helm and ran the throttle forward.

The 38-foot Tiara motored away from the pier and out into the Caribbean Sea. Following a few over-the-shoulder glances at the fiery scene—and seeing no one coming after her with a gun in his hand—Mercy Sands breathed a sigh of relief then ran a palm down her face, careful to stay away from her swollen eye and cheek. She glanced at the Tiara's controls, and her mind drifted to her younger years, to simpler times.

While her teenage girlfriends had been learning how to paint their nails, do their hair, and put on makeup, she had been learning how to fly planes and helicopters, as well as how to operate yachts. Thanks to her wealthy father, who had owned several expensive flying machines and watercraft, she now had the skills to navigate her way out of her current predicament.

Rubbing the back of her neck, Mercy cranked her head from side to side, the moves highlighting new pains, pains she didn't know she had. She closed her eyes for a moment, then sighed, her broken body longing for a hot shower, a cold beverage, and a week of sleep.

CHAPTER 3
A Different Person

The hollow ping of an aluminum bat, the thump of rawhide hitting rawhide, and the cheering from moms and dads in the stands were hallmark sounds of summer evenings across the heartland of America. And the summer league of competitive baseball in Iowa was in full swing.

At the plate, a freckle-faced and tanned 8-year-old boy, a lefty, got out ahead of an inside fastball—ping—sending a line drive over the outstretched glove of the first baseman.

In the bleachers near first base, a 35-year-old woman wearing a white tank-top, navy-blue shorts, sunglasses, and a blue denim ball hat leaped to her feet. Cupping her mouth with both hands, she hooted and hollered before clapping her hands and exchanging high fives with another woman nearby.

Rounding the bag at first, the hitter watched the right fielder gather the ball cleanly into his glove. The runner took a few steps toward second, making sure the throw to the shortstop wasn't high or wide, before he trotted back to the bag, a smile on his face as he stole a quick peek at his mother.

The woman in the tank-top twice pumped her fist at him before clapping again. A tick later, she adjusted her shirt while casting a backward glance, her mind thinking everyone behind her could see the crosshatching of scars on her back. She normally wore dark-colored shirts that came up to her neck, but today was just too dang hot and humid for those.

Shrugging off her paranoia, she spied her boy on first base. This was John's first year of competitive baseball. Last year, he had played in a recreational league, but he had become frustrated with his teammates. While he had been super focused on learning and practicing all the details of the game, they had been twirling their gloves in the outfield, watching butterflies, or picking boogers.

So, the transition to the competitive league had been an easy decision. And the right one. John was a baseball natural. In addition to having a knack for making contact with the ball at the plate, he also had a talent for pitching, even striking out kids one and two years older than he was.

"I have to say," said the woman who had high-fived 'Tank-Top,' "John can really hit the ball. You must be proud of him."

Mercy Sands beamed. To say mom was proud of her son would be an understatement. "And I take all the credit, too."

The woman laughed, as did Mercy, but the latter

mother hadn't completely meant what she had said as a joke. In high school, Mercy had been her fast-pitch softball team's starting pitcher, finishing her career with a .750 winning percentage. And as a hitter, she had knocked her fair share of pitches over the fence.

"Well, then maybe John *and* you can give my son some pointers."

Mercy chuckled. "We'd love to help out Sam."

"I can make hotdogs for the occasion. That's about the extent of *my* baseball wisdom."

The women shared another laugh before cheering again when the next hitter sent a looping ball into left field for a single.

John rounded second, raced toward third, then slid feet first into the bag a half second ahead of the tag. A billowing cloud of dust floated toward the third base dugout, as the umpire stretched out his arms toward his sides.

Mercy jumped up and down, screaming and clapping right along with the other parents around her.

· · ·

One Hour Later...

When the game had finished, and after a short team meeting, the coach had turned the kids loose. Now Mercy and John strolled across the parking lot.

"Did you see me slide into third, Mom?"

Mercy grinned. "I did."

"I hit the bag just as," John ran ahead of his mother to act out what had happened, "that kid was," he swung his glove across the dirt, "coming down with the ball."

Mercy's grin blossomed as she stared at her offspring, the love of her life. *If the baseball thing doesn't work out, he has a good shot at becoming an actor.*

"John," yelled a boy from somewhere.

Mercy and John turned toward the voice that ended up belonging to one of John's teammates.

The boy beckoned John with his arm. "Come on. Some of us are gonna play some pepper."

John looked up at his mother. "Can I go, Mom? Can I?"

Mercy made a face while going from her son to where a few of his teammates were gathering for the pepper game. "I don't know, John." She shook her head while eyeing the time on her watch. "I have to get up early for work tomorrow."

"Pleeease, Mom."

She shot a look at her car, came back to John, then frowned while turning her attention back toward her vehicle, her eyes narrowing when she spotted a man in a black suit leaning against a nearby black SUV. Her heart raced in her chest while sweat beads trickled down her back.

"Everyone's gonna be there, Mom."

Mercy didn't hear her son's pleas. Her thoughts were

lost in the past as she reached up over her left shoulder, the fingertips of her right hand touching the scars on her back. A tug on her arm brought her back to the present. She looked down at John.

"Just for a little bit, Mom. That's all."

Mercy glimpsed the man in black then nodded at her son. "Fifteen minutes. No more."

John bolted away from her.

She raised her voice. "And stay in the open where I—"

"Where you can see me," said John without turning around.

Mercy huffed, grinning as she shook her head at him. *Oh, David, honey. I wish you could see your son. You'd be so prou—* the thought of her deceased husband brought a tear to her eye as she swallowed the lump in her throat.

Fifteen months after Mercy's wedding, her husband had passed away. He was dead a month after initially seeing a doctor for a sudden pain in his side. One month from diagnosis to death. *Super cancer.* She wasn't sure if that had been the official medical term; however, there were six individuals at the funeral who knew, or knew of, someone who had succumbed to cancer within a similar time frame. And these people hadn't been smokers in their seventies or eighties. No. They had been healthy men and women in their twenties, thirties, or forties. *Super cancer.* Of all the words that had crossed Mercy's mind, 'super' had not been one she would have used to describe this disease, a disease that was seemingly on the rise; an illness that had taken her 31-year-old husband and left a 27-year-old woman alone, eight months away from the birth of her baby.

•••

Sauntering forward, Mercy squinted at the man in the black suit, white shirt, and navy-blue tie. He had gained weight around his midsection and had lost some hair, the setting sun illuminating skin beneath his thinning comb-over. As she approached, she could see perspiration forming on his chubby cheeks as well as a darker patch of moist fabric spreading across the front of his shirt.

The last time she had seen this man, he had been 'middle management' in Immigration and Customs Enforcement. That was a decade ago. She had no doubts he was now higher up the chain of command. During the years she had known him, worked for him, ambition had oozed from his pores. At the time, she had told herself to stay close to him, stay on his good side, and he would naturally take her along with him as he ascended the ranks. But all that went out the window after the incident in the Caribbean.

Mercy stopped six feet from her former boss, a man who back then had led a joint interagency task force (JITF) that had been commissioned to take down human

        FAR FROM MERCY

trafficking rings originating from Central America, Columbia, and Venezuela. And she had been one of his top agents, having infiltrated several criminal organizations and ultimately smuggling key information back to the task force, who would then orchestrate raids and round up the leaders and the henchmen.

"Mercy," said the man.

Standing near the SUV's left-front bumper, she looked across the hood at a second man. This one was dressed in a black suit and tie, too, but dark sunglasses shielded his full features, and his age, from her. Her eyes dipped to the man's plain, black oval belt buckle; a buckle large enough to draw a glance, but not ornate enough to warrant a detailed inspection.

"Your son is quite the ball player."

Mercy folded her arms across her chest and stared at her onetime superior.

He slid hands inside pants pockets, glimpsed the gravel ahead of his black shoes, then eyed her again. "I was at the funeral." Not getting a response, he added, "Your husband was a good man. I'm sorry for—"

"So, what do I call you these days, Terrance?" Mercy shifted her weight to her right foot. "Executive Associate Director Duval, *Deputy* Director Duval, or are you in charge of *everything* now at ICE?"

Duval half smiled. "Straight to business." He shook his head. "No, I'm still running the JITF. The trafficking of women and children up through Mexico and into the

US is still a thriving enterprise. And those above me," he paused, his right eye twitching once, "well, they seem to like me right where I'm at."

Surprised that his ambition had not landed him a cushy six-figure job with a corner office, Mercy quickly recovered, saying, "Too bad," hoping her I-don't-give-a-rat's-bleep tone had come through loud and clear. "Why are you here?"

"I have a proposal for you."

"Not interested."

"You *will* be when you hear it."

"If you're involved, I'll pass."

The five-ten, late fifties Duval scratched his cheek then intertwined his forearms in front of his chest. "Look, I know our working relationship didn't exactly end on the best of terms."

"The best of terms?" shot back Mercy, leaning closer to him while holding up two fingers. "*Twice* I told you I—"

The woman who had been sitting next to Mercy in the bleachers came up on Mercy's three o'clock, her son Sam with her.

Mercy gave her a wide smile. "See you at the next game, Carol." She waved at the boy. "Good game today, Sam."

"Thanks, Ms. Sands," the kid replied.

Carol turned around and caught Mercy's eye while walking backwards. "I'll call you to find a good time when you and John can come over for those," she poked a finger at her offspring, making sure he didn't see her, "pointers we talked about."

Mercy smiled again then nodded. "I'm looking forward to it."

Carol spun around and kept on going, Sam by her side.

When they were out of earshot, Mercy picked up where she had left off. "I *told* you I thought I had been made and needed extraction," she said through clenched teeth.

"It was a judgement call," said Duval.

"And your *judgement* left me strung up in a dirty basement."

"Not a day goes by I don't regret what happened."

"Well," Mercy threw up her arms, "as long as you're sorry, I guess we should just forget the whole thing, right?"

"At the time, we didn't have enough to roll up on Romero." Duval eyed her. "And I figured you could handle yourself," a beat, "Prodigal."

Mercy gave Duval an icy stare while slowly shaking her head at him. "I'm not *her* anymore." She glimpsed her son over her shoulder. "I'm a different person now."

He glimpsed the eight-year-old then came back to her. "Becoming a mother doesn't erase your past," a tick, "or keep you from doing what you're *still* capable of doing. It's in your blood."

She whipped her head toward him, "We're done here," then whirled around to leave.

"What about the proposal? Don't you want to know?"

Mercy kept on walking away.

"Romero has surfaced again."

Her gait hitched before her pace slowed.

Duval noticed. "I've been tasked with bringing him down." He cocked his head at her. "And I'm offering *you* the job."

Mercy took a few more steps then stopped to put her hands on her hips. After studying the ground for a bit, she pivoted to cut the distance between him and her in half. "Why? Why me? I'm sure you have many qualified candidates who can do that."

"I do," he replied. "But *you* have a history with him."

Mercy stiffened her back while barely rolling her shoulders, her mind envisioning Romero's handiwork etched all over her body.

"You know him better than anyone else on my task force." Duval raised a shoulder. "Plus, I figure I owe you one."

"Owe me?"

"Revenge," he said with a snarl.

"I told you. I'm not the same vengeful person you knew."

Fishing out a business card from a jacket pocket, "My number's the same, but in case you've forgotten," Duval held out the card.

Mercy didn't budge.

"I've been authorized to go as high as 250 grand for contractors. But I'm not haggling with you. If you want the job, it's yours for the whole two-fifty." After a few more seconds of standing there with his arm outstretched, he moseyed toward her vehicle's windshield and tucked his card under a wiper blade. "If you change your mind, call me. But don't wait too long. This is time sensitive. And if I don't hear from you, I'll be forced to move on to the next person." He then doled out a quick half smile and a dip of his chin. "Good to see you again, Mercy."

Without acknowledging him, she marched off to get her son.

Duval watched her go. A moment later, he sensed his sidekick on his right.

"Sir?" said the man.

"What is it?"

"You called her Prodigal. I don't remember reading anything about that in her personnel file."

Duval filled his lungs then exhaled loudly. "It was her call sign. I'm the one who gave it to her."

The other man nodded before squinting at a departing Mercy. "Is there some significance there?"

Duval took a moment to answer, his thoughts taking him back to more than a decade ago. "No matter how deep she became embedded, rubbing elbows with snakes and scorpions; or no matter what kind of *mess* she ended up falling into," he lifted a corner of his mouth and huffed, "Prodigal always found her way home."

TWO DAYS LATER

Mercy held her breath amidst the cloud of smoke swirling around her as she hauled a pan from the oven and quickly set it on the counter. In the other room, a smoke alarm blared. She picked up a towel and whipped her way through the gray haze to kick the oven door shut.

In the backyard, outside the kitchen, oblivious to his mother's culinary tribulations, her son John tossed a baseball into the air and caught it in his glove. The summer heat had not let up, but he didn't care. Sweaty and stinky, he kept on heaving the ball into the air and snatching it on the way down.

Coughing, Mercy ditched her oven mitts to step onto a chair and disassemble the smoke alarm. Once the noise had stopped, she surveyed the charred remains of tonight's dinner—a blackened roast with burned potatoes and sweet carrots that were now heavily 'glazed.' It might be possible to salvage the carrots, but with everything smelling like smoke, none of it was appetizing anymore.

The forty-year-old oven had been acting up for the last couple of months. 'Too old to get parts for it,' the guy at the hometown appliance store had told her. And a new oven would have definitely blown up her budget. So, she had gotten by with adjusting the temperature and the cooking times. This evening, however, the thing had decided to go 'nuclear,' ramping all the way up to who knows how high. High enough to ruin dinner and prompt Mercy to reach for the phone to order a pizza.

"Half an hour?" she said. "Sounds good." Clicking off, she put her hands on the edge of the sink and stared at her debacle. *Good money literally down the drain.*

Doing a one-eighty to lean back against the sink, she held her head in her hand for a few moments before folding her arms across her belly and giving her seventy-year-old, two-bedroom country home a look. The small, out-of-date kitchen also doubled as a dining room with a two-person table and two wooden chairs in one corner. Through the archway, a slightly bigger room, the living room, met up with a short hallway, a bathroom and the two bedrooms branching off from it.

She thought of the basement, which had a low ceiling, a cracked concrete floor, and walls in need of paint, along with some repairs to a few mortar joints. Centered in that dank space, a relatively new furnace shared the wide-open level with a washer and dryer that sat in one corner, both of those appliances having been purchased secondhand a few years ago and, like the oven, were now showing signs they too were getting ready to give up the ghost.

When Mercy first moved to Iowa and signed the

mortgage for this place, when John was two, things hadn't been so difficult. Her job at the diner had been enough to pay the bills and provide her and her son with a decent existence. She had even managed to build up an emergency fund. Then, three years ago, something called inflation had crept into her life—into the lives of every American in fact—and now, with that emergency fund exhausted, she found herself relying more and more on credit cards to make ends meet.

She spied the phone she held, Duval's voice in her head. *My number's the same.* Mercy had torn up and tossed into the trash his business card the minute she had gotten home that night. Lifting her head, she watched John pound the baseball into his glove. *250 grand would go a long way toward his college fund. If that's what he wanted to do, that is.* She could set aside half for college and still have enough to give him a better life in the here and now.

Mercy hung her head, thoughts of her previous occupation rushing back to her, thoughts she had tried to bury. It was true. She was a different person today than she had been back when she was deep undercover, living among psychotic killers, rapists, child molesters, the worst of the worst.

In the beginning, the vile things she had witnessed had turned her stomach. Little by little, however, those things had become commonplace, her senses, her humanity, dulled to the point where she no longer saw those acts for what they were...pure evil. She had been willing to pay that price, however, to serve her country, to bring gang lords to justice and to save innocent women and children from being abused, sold into sexual slavery.

In the end, though, she had taken a measure of solace in the acts of violence she herself had perpetrated. Whether she saw what she had done as justice, revenge, or therapy, she wasn't certain. Maybe all three. All she knew for sure was that pulling the trigger on those criminals had come awfully easy to her. And even though she had felt her soul slipping further and further away, deeper and deeper into darkness, she kept on dropping bodies.

Mercy now eyed the phone in her hand. She didn't need Duval's business card. His number had been seared into her memory. The mid-thirties mother gave her son another long look, watching him play. She closed her eyes and filled her lungs before letting her head fall. "Oh, God," she said under her breath, "talk to me. What do I do? Let me hear Your voice."

Seconds later, she lumbered into the living room, plopped onto the sofa, and opened a Bible app on her phone. *Speak to me, Lord. I need You.*

•••

Twenty Minutes Later...
After reading different Scripture passages for the last

twenty minutes, Mercy now found herself immersed in Matthew: *"Go and learn the meaning of the words, 'I desire mercy, not sacrifice.' I did not come to call the righteous but sinners."* This verse held a special place in her heart.

Lifting her eyes to spy the wooden crucifix on the wall across the room, Mercy recalled that day from six years ago. She had just finished a ten-hour shift at work. Tired, sweaty, and looking like a wet rag, she was on her way to pick up John from daycare. Waiting at a stoplight, she had glanced up and spotted a billboard with a Bible verse some religious organization had posted on it—Matthew 9:13—and seeing those words, specifically her name in print, had hit her square in the chest.

Growing up, Mercy had not been particularly religious. Sure, her parents had gone to church, mostly at Christmas and Easter, dragging their daughter along as well, but their faith wasn't very deep.

Mercy stared at the crucifix, but her mind was years in the past. That day had been hot—mid-nineties—and the air conditioning in her car wasn't working. Adding to her misery, the heat coming off the pavement felt like she had opened the door to the oven and peeked too quickly at whatever was baking inside. But when she read the verse on that billboard, it seemed as if the day's troubles didn't matter. It was as if God Himself had been speaking to her, saying to her, 'I see you, and you are mine.'

She ran her thumb down her phone's screen, scrolling up to the words, 'I desire mercy.' Her heart fluttered, as it always did, when she took in this part of the verse. Few people get to see their name in the Bible. Yes, she had discovered the Biblical context of the word was complex, with many meanings—forgiveness, compassion, kindness—but she couldn't help herself from seeing the 'M' as being capitalized.

She ran her thumb upward. *Not sacrifice.* This is where things became dicey. Closing her eyes, she saw the faces of all the people she had killed in the line of duty. Most of the acts had been justified, but some were not, and her spirit withered, as it always did, from the sudden realization of all the lives she had taken, sacrificed unjustly.

Mercy's eyes settled on the last part of the verse. This part brought hope back into her soul. *I did not come to call the righteous but sinners.* She swallowed. *Sinners.* For years, that word had stung, pierced her heart. Each time she saw it; it was as if the lance that had pierced Jesus' side had been thrust between her own ribs. She was a sinner. That was for sure. But at some point, she started focusing on the first half of the sentence. And gradually, she began to see that Jesus had come to earth specifically for those like her—sinners—and a quiet calm, an inner peace would fall over her each time she inwardly recited the second half of that Bible verse.

Mercy closed her eyes and drew in a big breath, holding it for a few beats, before slowly letting it out. *I did not come to call the righteous but sinners.* Like so many

     FAR FROM MERCY

times in the past, a serene comfort enveloped her, like the feeling of a warm blanket being draped around her body on a cold winter's night.

"When's dinner, Mom? I'm hungry."

Startled, Mercy opened her eyes and saw John standing beside the couch. *He's like a mini ninja or something.*

Still wearing his hat, he threw a baseball a couple feet into the air before catching it in his glove. "What smells in here? It smells like that time we had a fire in the backyard and roasted marshmallows. You remember that time, Mom? That was cool."

In her mind, lining up her 'roasted' dinner with the smell of the backyard fire he had mentioned, she raised a corner of her lip. *You're not that far off.* She spied the clock on the wall, stood, and shooed him toward the bathroom. "Yes, I remember that time. Now go wash up. Dinner's almost ready."

"What are we having?" he said over his shoulder while being nudged down the hallway.

"Pizza."

"Ooh," he pumped a fist, "yes!"

"I figured you'd like that. Now go get cleaned up." Watching him skip down the hall before disappearing into the bathroom, Mercy smiled and shook her head. *You goof.* The smile vanished in the next instant when she raised her phone. *250 grand. College tuition. A better life here and now.* Following a big sigh, she dialed a number.

A man answered. "Duval."

Grimacing, at the notion of being dragged back into the life she had left behind, she drew her lips into her mouth and held her forehead.

Three seconds passed.

"Mercy? Is that you?"

It's only one job, she thought, *and then I'm out for good.* "Yeah, it," she faltered, "it's me." Biting her lower lip, she made a fist and ground her fingers into her palm, subconsciously rubbing off the slime that wasn't there, as she saw herself shaking hands with the devil. "I'm in."

Mercy sat on her haunches on her friend Carol's front porch, straightening her son John's t-shirt, a t-shirt he had somehow managed to get dirty in the short drive from the house to here. She drank in his black hair, freckled face, sparkling blue eyes, and square jaw, all of which he had gotten from his father, before she glimpsed the ball hat on his head and the baseball glove tucked under his arm. *You may look like your dad, but your throwing and hitting talents are all me*, she thought with an inward smile.

"Why do you have to go, Mom?"

Mercy's heart broke at the anxiety in his voice. He didn't do well with change; a trait she was sure had been passed on from her genes. *Maybe my leaving will be good for him, help him to see that change can be a positive thing.* She heard her words and pressed her lips together at her failed attempt at soothing her own guilt.

"Don't you worry," she replied, while cupping his shoulders. "I should only be away for a couple of days, three at the most."

John hung his head.

Feeling his shoulders slump, Mercy lifted his head with a curled forefinger under his chin. "Hey."

A moment later, he raised his eyes to meet hers.

"When have I ever lied to you, huh?" She smiled even though her heart was dropping into her twisted gut. "Haven't I always been honest with you?"

He bobbled his head a bit before nodding.

"I'll be back before you know it." Mercy glimpsed Carol, who was standing in the archway, hovering behind the boy, before she came back to him. "And in the meantime, you're going to have a blast with Carol and Sam."

"That's right," said a smiling Carol, leaning forward to see the side of his face. "We're going to do all kinds of fun things together—baseball, cookouts, maybe even a trip down to the water. Doesn't that sound like fun?"

John looked up at the woman then faced his mother.

Mercy noticed a glimmer of hope cross his features. She drew him closer. "Give me hugs."

He laid limp arms on her hips.

Embracing his listless body, she tickled him. "You can do better than that."

He squirmed and giggled before squeezing her midsection.

"That's it." She gripped him a bit tighter then stood, keeping him at arm's length while peering down at him. "You be a good boy for Mrs. Lyons, okay?"

He nodded.

        FAR FROM MERCY

"I love you."

"Love you, too."

Mercy spied Carol.

Carol smiled. "I'll take good care of him."

Mercy swallowed then nodded a few times. "Thank you for doing this. I'm so sorry for dropping this on you on such short notice."

"It's no trouble at all." The homeowner glanced down. "John is *always* welcome here."

Mercy gave her son another look and sniffed. She had left him at daycare while she had gone to work; later, with teachers in the public school system. But those times she had been in the same town as her boy. This time, however, she would be flying to another country.

She kissed him on the cheek, "Bye, John," stepped off the porch, and walked away, conscious of how heavy her legs were, how the simple act of putting one foot in front of the other seemed so difficult. It was like that time in the hospital, after she had just had surgery, and the nurses were forcing her to get out of bed and get moving. She didn't want to do it, but she knew it was for the best.

Following a wave back at the house, she climbed behind the wheel of her older-model, two-door white Honda Civic and drove away while looking out the passenger window, waving at her son.

Tears flowing, she toughed it out until the Civic rounded the corner at the first block. Once out of sight of the house, she pulled over to dry her eyes and wait for the waterworks to stop.

•••

One Hour Later...
Maple City Municipal Airport
Maple City, Iowa

Dressed in blue jeans, a sleeves-rolled-up-to-the-elbows, open-front light-blue dress shirt over a white tank-top, and brown-and-tan hiking boots, her long blonde hair fluttering in the wind, Mercy fast walked across the tarmac, pulling a rolling suitcase behind her with a carry-on slung over her left shoulder.

Up ahead, shimmering in the sun, a white-with-blue-trim Beechcraft King Air 350 sat with its stairs down and engines running, a man in khaki pants and a white short-sleeved polo shirt standing by the staircase.

Approaching the aircraft, Mercy removed her metal-framed, gold-colored black sunglasses and tucked them into her shirt pocket. As best as she could, she had made peace with leaving her son in the care of another woman. Now it was time to focus on the mission, on what needed to be done to bring Nestor Romero to justice.

"Ms. Sands," said the man.

She recognized him from the baseball game, mostly by the sunglasses and the large, unadorned oval belt buckle he wore. He had been with Duval.

Standing a couple inches shy of six feet tall, he took

off his sunglasses and extended his right hand. "It's a pleasure to formally make your acquaintance. Agent Walt Freeman—Immigration and Customs Enforcement."

Without the glasses obstructing his features, Mercy estimated him to be in his mid-twenties as she took in his short, dark-brown hair, wide 'squinty' eyes, broad nose, and pointed chin. She shook his hand. "I was expecting your boss."

"Mister Duval was forced to attend to other matters. He sends his regards. May I?" Freeman gestured toward Mercy's carry-on.

She slid the strap off her shoulder.

He shouldered the bag and hefted her rolling suitcase. "The jet's gassed up and ready to go, so," he stepped aside, "after you, Ms. Sands."

"Call me Mercy." She ascended the staircase ahead of Freeman. "How long have you worked for Terrance?"

"Three months."

She stepped into the plane to see it was void of people. "And ICE?"

He stowed her luggage and faced her. "*Six* months."

Mercy gave him a down-and-up while frowning.

He raised his hands in surrender. "Don't worry. I've been told that you're the one in charge of this operation. My role is purely a supporting one, liaising with ICE to make sure you have whatever you need."

Nodding, she eyed the empty seats. "Where's the rest

of the team?”

“Thirty-six to forty-eight hours behind us.”

Mercy half closed an eye at him. “That’s not how we used to do it when I was with the task force. We all went in *together*.”

Freeman shrugged. “I can’t speak to the past. What I *can* speak to, though, is that Mr. Duval is ironing out some personnel issues and that you and I are to conduct reconnaissance once we land in Honduras. Then, when everyone is in-country, we’ll—sorry,” he pointed at her, “*you’ll* prep the team and plan the rendition.”

Mercy studied her ICE liaison. The op wasn’t off to the start she had envisioned. Then again, ten years is a long time. Things change. She half chuckled to herself. There was that word again. *Change.* She thought of her son and how anxiety would creep into him whenever his young life didn’t go as planned. *Like mother, like son.*

“So, if you’re ready,” Freeman hooked a thumb toward the cockpit, “I’ll go tell the pilot we’re ready for takeoff.”

Her mind spinning from the last-minute alterations, Mercy strolled toward the right-rearmost seat and sat down facing the nose of the aircraft. “Yeah, I’m ready.” She found her seatbelt. “Let’s get this thing in the air.”

SEVEN HOURS LATER
RAMÓN VILLEDA MORALES INTERNATIONAL AIRPORT
SAN PEDRO SULA, HONDURAS

Having exited the air-conditioned airport to make her way to the parking lot, and the car waiting for her and Freeman, Mercy fanned her shirt a few times. She had left behind the low nineties' temps and cloudy skies of Iowa for San Pedro Sula's upper nineties, clear skies, and oppressive humidity. Great conditions for a day at the beach in your bikini. But not that great when long pants, shirts, and heavy shoes are the requirement of the day. Thankfully, a light breeze was cutting some of the stickiness.

Mercy shoved her suitcase and carry-on into the back of an older-model, light-gray four-door Hyundai Tucson then backed away to inspect the compact crossover SUV sporting some dirt and light dents in places. The small vehicle, which had been dropped off for the duo by one of ICE's local assets in Honduras, was perfect for blending in with local traffic.

Freeman pulled down on the rear hatch before pushing to slam it shut.

Mercy climbed into the front passenger seat and reached behind her to drag a duffle bag onto the center console.

Freeman got in behind the steering wheel, fired up the car, and cranked the A/C to high.

She ran the zipper on the bag and hauled out a Glock G19 pistol, two spare magazines, and holsters for the gun and mags.

Freeman claimed his own G19 and gear and started donning the equipment. "Do you want to check in at the hotel first or drive out to Romero's?"

Now 'strapped,' Mercy pulled back on her Glock's slide a hair, to verify a round was in the chamber, then holstered the nine-millimeter and retrieved her cell phone. "Neither."

He cocked his head. "*Where* then?"

"I already know the layout of Romero's villa." She tapped her phone's screen several times then put the device to her face. "Spent a lot of time there. Don't need to see it again."

"Okay, so then—"

Mercy held up a forefinger and spoke into her mobile. "Hola, Padre. It's me...Mercy."

•••

One Hour Later...

An hour from sunset, with daylight disappearing quickly behind a nearby tree line, Mercy and Freeman stood at the back door of a small structure with a conical-shaped, four-sided roof that led to a spire at the top.

After leaving the airport, Freeman had driven while Mercy had doled out directions. She finished by telling him to take a single-lane road that was easy to miss if you weren't looking for it.

Parking the Hyundai in dense woods, the two had then traversed an overgrown path through the trees to where they now waited.

The back door opened, and a late-fifties, dark-skinned man with thinning gray hair and black eyeglasses stood in the darkened doorway. He gave Freeman a wary glance then eyed Mercy.

She nodded. "He's okay."

The five-eight, rail-thin man, wearing a black suit, white shirt, and Roman collar, swung open the door and beckoned them. When his guests were inside, he scanned the woods, shut the door, then faced the newcomers, specifically the female one, a broad smile dawning on his rugged, weathered features. "Mercy." He spread his arms wide. "It's been a long time, my child."

The two embraced.

"How have you been?" he asked.

"Good, Padre. Good."

He held on for a few seconds longer, then let go. Holding her at arm's length, "Let me see you," he took in every square inch of her face and hair. "Still beautiful as ever, I see."

Blushing, she returned the compliment with a genuine smile. "And you still look like you could," she held up her fists, "go ten rounds in the ring with anyone."

The holy man laughed. "I wish that were true." His attention veered left.

Mercy glanced to her right. "This is Walt Freeman. He works for ICE." She motioned toward her host. "Meet Jorge Montoya. He's the priest here at Saint John's."

The men clasped hands and exchanged pleasantries.

"So," said Montoya, "does this mean you are back with ICE?"

Mercy shook her head. "Not officially. This is more like a," she paused, "a subcontractor job. One and done."

"Ah," the Episcopalian priest nodded then smiled at her. "I was beginning to think I'd never see you again. This is such a blessing."

Mercy grinned while reaching out to take his hand. "It's wonderful to see you doing so well. How is your family?"

"Oh, Luisa is the love of my life, and the kids are now grown and living their own lives."

Mercy saw a twinkle in his eye. She could see he was bursting to tell her something. "And?"

"And," he beamed, "my Lili's married now."

Mercy's eyebrows shot upward as an image of Montoya's daughter, 10-years-old the last time Mercy had seen the girl, flashed across her mind. "Little Lili?"

Montoya nodded several times. "Sí, she has a terrific

          FAR FROM MERCY

husband, a two-year-old daughter, and another girl on the way."

"Oh my," Mercy held a hand to her mouth before patting his hand. "You must be one proud abuelo."

The happy grandfather raised his hands and eyed the ceiling. "Children are a gift from the Lord." He came back to Mercy. "And like arrows in the hand of a warrior, blessed is the man who has filled his quiver with them."

"Amen," she replied.

"And you?" asked Montoya. "Do you have little ones at home?"

"A son. His name's John, and he's," her gaze drifted off for a beat before settling on her friend from her past, "like my Lord and Savior, he's my everything."

"I know what you mean, my child. I know what you mean." Montoya summoned them. "This way." He led the trio down a couple short hallways and into the church's main gathering area. "I've sent everyone home for the day, and all the doors are locked. We are alone."

Mercy glanced at the raised sanctuary off to her right. A large wooden crucifix faced the main doors at the opposite end of the structure. Tile flooring throughout, the space had two large seating areas of wooden pews down the middle with two smaller sections flanking the large areas. In addition to two stained-glass windows set into the walls on either side of the main entrance, holy images and murals adorned the walls with potted flowers positioned here and there.

Up above, metal beams supported a corrugated metal roof. Cut into different parts of the roof, rectangular sky lights let in natural light. Even now, with the overhead tubular-style light fixtures off, the setting sun's rays still reflected off the metal roof's shiny surface, lighting up the church's interior. Finally, four ceiling fans slowly turned, moving the air, and keeping the inside temperature quite pleasant.

Montoya claimed territory on the first-row pew.

Mercy sat on his right and pivoted toward him.

Freeman remained standing, so he could face the two.

"After we spoke earlier," said Montoya, "I made a few calls to some of my people." He crossed his left leg over his right and rotated toward Mercy. "It seems Nestor Romero arrived in Honduras two weeks ago. He's been keeping a low profile for much of that time."

"And when he's not?" prompted Mercy.

Montoya smiled. "You were right. My sources tell me he's made appearances at two different nightclubs in San Pedro Sula."

"Which ones?"

He gave her the names. "He was there last—"

"I'm sorry to interrupt," interjected Freeman, "but who are these sources, these people you keep referring to?"

The holy man eyed Mercy. "Haven't you told him of our previous work together?"

She raised a shoulder, "Didn't think he needed to

know," before facing her ICE liaison. "I met Jorge a good dozen years ago. One of the girls in Romero's entourage had gotten messed up by a couple of his guys at this nightclub. At some point during the night, I slipped out the back door to contact my handler when I found her lying in an alley behind the club. Not sure what to do, I remembered hearing rumors about," Mercy came back to Montoya, "this priest at a local church..."

Montoya grinned at her.

"...who I was told had a reputation for taking in people, caring for them, and possibly getting them out of the country."

"Why not just call the police or an ambulance?" asked Freeman.

Montoya looked up at his male counterpart. "Sex workers in Honduras are not looked upon favorably. Because of what these individuals do, the police, who are sometimes working with the cartels and gangs, won't investigate the assaults. And the hospitals do what they can, but when the victim has no insurance and no money to pay the bill," Montoya let his words hang in the air.

Freeman looked away, a grimace overtaking his features. "Nice."

"Part of the problem is the machismo culture here in Central America," added Mercy. "Women and children are viewed as less important than men." A beat. "So, I ended up taking this young girl I found to," she raised a hand and glanced around, "here, where I met Jorge for the first time. He cared for the girl and eventually got her out of the sex industry."

"And for the next couple of years," Montoya reached out to lay a hand on her shoulder, "*you* helped me smuggle another dozen or so women out of the sex trade and out of the country."

Mercy huffed. "That's nothing compared to the hundreds, maybe even the thousands, you've rescued."

"Just like the parable of the lost sheep, there is more joy in Heaven over," he raised a finger, "one saved sinner, a saved life. Make no mistake, Mercy. God sees you. He sees the good you've done."

She bounced her eyebrows, her mind quicker to recall her misdeeds than her good deeds. "I hope you're right, Padre." She poked her chin at him. "When was Romero last seen out in public?"

"Last Saturday."

She stared at the altar on the elevated sanctuary. "Today's Friday, so he'll be itching to get out either tonight or tomorrow. Maybe *both* nights."

"What does any of that have to do with our primary mission?" asked Freeman.

Mercy turned her head toward him. "We have a chance to nab Romero without having to raid his home, without having to fire a single shot."

He crossed arms over his chest and waited.

"I know Romero," she continued. "I know his usual haunts, the nightclubs he frequents. All we have to do is stakeout the club he'll be going to. When he arrives, I get close to him, separate him from his security team, and," she dipped her forehead toward Freeman, "the two of us kidnap him and then deliver him to," before facing Montoya, "you...for transport."

Montoya thought. "I can have him on a plane and," he eyed her, "flown to the United States, I presume?"

She nodded. "Where he'll be tried for his crimes; specifically, the human trafficking of women and children."

"I like it," said the holy man. "It could work. I know of a small airfield—and a *pilot* who would be willing to—"

"Duval signed off on a *raid* of Romero's villa," said Freeman.

"And am I, or am I *not*, in charge of this entire field operation?" countered Mercy.

"You are, but—"

"Then I have the authority to make changes."

"What about the rest of the team?"

"You said they're forty-eight hours behind us. If this goes as planned, we'll be flying home before they even leave the States."

Freeman frowned. "Aren't you forgetting one crucial element? Romero knows who you are, knows what you look like."

"It's been ten years. People change." Mercy waved him off. "Let me worry about that." She faced Montoya. "How soon can you have that plane ready to take off?"

He scratched his chin. "If the pilot I'm thinking of is still in Chamelecón, not long. I'd have to make a call."

"Make contact and see if he can be ready by midnight."

Montoya retrieved his cell phone.

"Let me know what you find out, will you, Padre?"

"Sí."

Mercy stood and squared shoulders with Freeman. "In the meantime, you and I need to plan escape routes from two different nightclubs to," she hooked a thumb toward the priest, "the airfield where that plane will be waiting for us."

"You're really serious about this, aren't you, the two of us kidnapping a ruthless cartel leader surrounded by who knows how many armed guards?"

"I am." She noted the concern etched on his face. "Don't forget. We have the advantage. I know this man. I've seen him in action. I know his tastes, his motivations, how he thinks."

Freeman wrung the back of his neck for a few seconds, sighed, then hauled out his phone. "All right. I'll update Duval."

She covered his hand, the hand holding his mobile. "No."

Freeman eyed her. "He's my superior. He needs to—"

"Trust me. I'll make sure he knows you were following *my* orders. You won't get in trouble." A beat. "Now, come on. We need to make some stops before the stores close."

8:54 P.M.

After parting ways with Jorge Montoya, Mercy and Freeman had gone shopping for clothes, shoes, a wig, everything she would need for the operation to capture Nestor Romero. Mercy now slid her hands around the back of her neck and raised the black, curly, long-haired wig she wore while twisting her body to see the back of herself in her hotel room's full-length mirror.

The sleeveless royal-blue, ruched, high-neck satin dress followed the curves of her bust, hips, and knees before flaring out at her ankles, mimicking the look of an elegant, prom-like evening dress. A slit on each side— from the knees down—showed off brief glimpses of skin as well as her footwear.

After letting her faux hair fall to the middle of her back, Mercy spread apart the right slit to eye her black four-inch, high-heeled gladiator sandals with leather straps crisscrossing up her calves and stopping at a narrow, black leather belt encircling her leg just above her knee. *If this doesn't get Romero's attention, then he's either gone blind or—*

"Mind if I ask you a personal question?" said

Freeman.

"You can certainly *ask*," she replied while turning toward the mirror to tease the 'springy' curls that fell around her temples and cheeks, making sure they disguised most of her features, features that had been heavily altered with eye shadow, lipstick, blush, everything she could throw at them, so she didn't look like the Mercy Sands Romero had known. "Not guaranteeing any answers, though."

"Why'd you leave ICE?"

"Personal reasons."

He huffed at the circular nature of her answer. "Was it Duval?"

Mercy spied Freeman's reflection. "What makes you say that?"

"Because the tension at the ball field that day was heavier than the air itself. Plus, I know what happened to you, the mission in the Caribbean."

"Well," she adjusted her dress at the hips, "it seems you've done your homework on me, Agent Freeman."

"Not really. You're something of a," he paused, "a mini legend at the agency. People still talk about you—what you *did*. Your accomplishments, shall we say...the bad actors you helped put away. Rather, I should say played a *major role* in putting away."

"The way I see it, *everyone* played a major role."

"Do you feel he betrayed you?" asked Freeman.

Mercy stopped primping to consider his query.

"Duval? No. No, he wouldn't betray me. He may be ambitious and self-serving, but he's no traitor." She went back to her physical prepping. "But he *was* making some bad decisions at the time, decisions that were risking the lives of good people."

"So, that's why you left?"

"Partly."

"Partly?" replied Freeman.

Spinning to face him, she laid her right hand on her right hip, a gold-colored bracelet sliding from her forearm to her wrist. "Do you have kids, Agent Freeman?"

He shook his head.

"A girlfriend? Wife?"

"I've been seeing someone for a year now."

She picked up a long, gold-colored teardrop earring and pushed the curved hook through the hole in her left earlobe. "And have you two ever talked about marriage, family, having kids?"

He bobbled his head from side to side. "The topic's come up a few times."

"Well," she hung an identical earring from her right earlobe, "speaking from experience, becoming a parent makes you aware of things you were never aware of before. You suddenly realize you're not living for yourself any longer, doing what you want, when you want. You have another life to care for, provide for, *be there* for."

He half rolled his eyes. "So I've heard."

"As had I." She lifted a finger toward him. "And like you just did, I rolled my eyes at people who used to tell me how having children had changed their lives. Didn't believe it. That is until I held my own helpless little infant in my hands for the first time. *Then* I believed it."

"So, to answer your question," placing a flat hand on her chest, her royal-blue fingernails matching the color of her dress, Mercy gave her getup a last look in the mirror. Her eyes settled on the dainty gold chain laying on her dress and beautifully contrasting with the garment's deep blue hues, "I left ICE partly because of Duval, but *mostly* because I wanted a family more than I wanted a big-time career."

He thought. "And somehow you can't have *both*?"

"Sure. I suppose. For me, though, I came to understand family was more important than a career. I didn't want to be away from them for months at a time in some country most people couldn't find on a map. I wanted to be home at five, spending the rest of the evening with those closest to me."

Freeman glanced away to gaze out the window.

Mercy noticed him, seemingly taking her words to heart. "Speaking of which," she snatched her phone from off the bed, "I need to make a call. Do you mind bringing the car around? I'll be out in five."

He nodded, "See you downstairs," then left the hotel room.

Mercy dialed a number, sat on a couch, and crossed

her legs at the knee, her dress splaying to show off her gladiator sandals. "Hello, Carol," she said while covering herself up, a wave of self-consciousness coming over her at the thought of her son seeing her in such an outfit. "It's Mercy. Is John still up?" She waited. "Thanks." Seconds later, the sound of her boy's voice produced a wide smile on her face. "Hey there, my little man. How ya' doing?"

"Okay," replied John.

"You and Sam having fun?"

"Uh-huh."

Still smiling, Mercy shook her head at the room's beige shag carpeting. If the conversation didn't involve baseball, getting him to open up was like catching a greased pig at the county fair. At least that's what other folks had said when referencing a hard task. And without having tried to catch a greased pig at any of the fairs she and John had gone to in the last few years, who was she to doubt them? "What'd you do today? Play any baseball?"

"Yeah," he said. "Me and Sam and some other kids in the neighborhood tossed around the ball. Mom, you should have seen me. I made this catch that…"

Mercy sunk deeper into the couch cushion, her smile somehow growing even bigger. She had said the magic word, and he was off and running, the excitement in his voice amping up a few notches. "Is that right? Well, tell me a-a-all about it."

• • •

Three Hours Later...
19 July—12:25 A.M.
San Pedro Sula

Located on the north end of the city, near Highway CA-13, the two-story nightclub was buzzing with activity, had been for hours. Revelers danced, gyrated, and waved their arms to loud music thumping from speakers hidden by low lighting and a haze of smoke being pumped across the dance floor. At one end, a DJ mixed tunes ranging from the Reggaeton genre to Dance to Electronic. A long, dark-colored bar at the opposite end of the floor had several mixologists stationed behind it, the mixologists serving drinks and taking payment.

Overhead spotlights crisscrossed the club, bathing the tightly packed throng of young people in multiple colors—pinks, blues, reds. Square, black, backless cushioned chairs were grouped throughout the first floor. Lounge areas, made up of leather, armless sofas with a small table between them, were located around the perimeter.

The second floor was a U-shaped loft area that overlooked the dance floor on three sides. Chairs and bistro tables lined the railings. In two corners, floor-to-ceiling stainless-steel poles were situated among more armless sofas. The third corner was a roped-off VIP section where a couple of the chairs near the railing had a view of the entire nightclub.

With clubbers crowding around her, Mercy sat on a

backless red stool at the bar, her right forearm on the bar's faux, wood-grained surface, her fingers slowly spinning a long-stemmed glass. Inside the martini glass was some fruity alcoholic beverage she had no intention of drinking. Every few minutes, she sipped to sell her role as a woman looking for a good time. In fact, over the last two hours, she had turned down four advances.

Sitting with her right leg crossed over her left, the heel of her left gladiator sandal hooked on the stool's lower rung, she made sure to show off enough of her legs to draw Romero's attention without screaming 'easy.' She knew his tastes in women. He preferred classy, subtle, and suggestive to tacky, indecent, and sleazy. And in an ocean of revealing miniskirts, low-cut tops, and sky-high heels, Mercy's concealing, elegant dress put her squarely in the camp of classiness.

She touched her drink to her lips then returned the vessel to the bar, her eyes taking in one woman's black patent leather thigh boots. Knowing the air was still muggy outside—and not too much better inside—Mercy inwardly shook her head while visualizing the young girl later on peeling off the boots, tipping them upside down, and watching the sweat pour out.

In Mercy's right ear, a wireless Bluetooth earpiece rested there, paired with the cell phone she carried. Anyone seeing it would think she was simply listening to music or on a phone call. The earpiece came alive.

Walt Freeman's voice: "There's still time to back out.

Romero might not even show tonight. It's getting late."

Mercy gave the nightclub another look; specifically, the main door, hoping to see her target come promenading in with his goons and girls. He was known to arrive later in the evening, when the club was packed, so everyone noticed him. She spied her watch, admitting to herself that his window to make an appearance was quickly closing.

"Plus," continued Freeman, who was sitting in their Hyundai Tucson outside the club, "the team will be coming in later today or tomorrow. We can get some sleep then take the rest of the day to scout Romero's villa, plan the attack."

"We'll give it fifteen more minutes."

"That's what you," two seconds passed, "you said fifteen minutes ago," replied Freeman, his words broken by a quick yawn.

Mercy thought about Agent Walt Freeman. He was young; young, strong, and eager for action. She knew well the thirst for action. That was what had motivated her to accept Terrance Duval's invitation to join his task force in the first place. As soon as he had said she would be in the thick of things, she was sold.

Now, however, looking back on her tenure with the task force, through the eyes of maturity and faith—and dare she say through the softening of motherhood—Mercy understood there was more to being an ICE agent than kicking in doors and hopefully getting the chance to shoot a human trafficker. Even now, sitting on a bar stool, amped up on a slow trickle of adrenaline, and poised for action, she was more than willing to do whatever was necessary to apprehend Nestor Romero; however, if that could be accomplished without bloodshed, then that was the better option. The fewer the people who had to die, the better. *I desire mercy, not sacrifice.* Those words had been rooted deep into Mercy Sands' soul. And she had no intention of abandoning them.

Mercy checked her watch—12:39. Her hopes of taking down Romero peacefully were fading faster and faster with every minute that passed.

...

12:46 A.M.

"Belay that order," said Mercy, getting back up on her bar stool. "Target is on site. I repeat, target is on site." Having told Freeman to 'pack it up' ten seconds ago, she now crossed her legs at the knee and opened the left slit on her dress. She glimpsed Romero.

Surrounded by attractive young women, his security detail encircling him and the women, Nestor Romero strode into the club, smiling and nodding at those he knew.

Mercy's insides quivered. It had been a long time since she had seen the man. She guessed him to be in his mid-fifties by now. His hairline had gotten higher, and his dark hair, slicked back into a pompadour, had grayed some at the sides. Even his scruffy beard had a fair amount of 'snow' in it. All of which surprised her. As vain as the man was, she would have thought he would've done something to fight off the aging process.

At six-one, and a hundred and ninety pounds, the Guatemalan, a giant in his native homeland, where the average male was only five-three, stood almost a full 'head' above most everyone in this Honduran nightclub.

Romero wore khaki pants and a short-sleeved Hawaiian shirt unbuttoned to his navel. The 'grays' hadn't quite made it south yet, as a large gold crucifix, hanging from a gold chain around his neck, mixed with his thick mane of black curly chest hair.

Mercy gritted her teeth as she watched him keep two women close to him, a shaggy arm coiled around each one's midsection. Most people would see that as a power move. She knew better. Those women were there in case one of his rivals sent someone to assassinate him. If an enemy hitman somehow made it past his guards, then he wanted his human shields to take a bullet for him.

Romero and his entourage ascended the staircase and fanned out in the VIP section, Romero himself taking a chair next to the handrail on his left. With his back to a wall, and his forearms resting on the handrail, he scanned the people below, from the stage to his right to the bar directly beneath him.

While pretending to watch the people dance, her drink in hand, Mercy kept an eye on him. When his gaze fell upon the bar area, she looked up at him, offered up a sultry half smile, then turned away to sip her beverage and return to observing the dancers.

For the next half minute, she spied him in her peripheral vision. He hadn't looked away. Placing her drink on the bar, she lightly bounced her leg, the act causing her dress to spread apart a little more, exposing more of her leg. It was a covert act, one that showed a glimpse of something hidden. Most young, immature women would have made some outright lewd motion, all the while virtually begging for attention from the man they had in their sights.

The middle school cat-and-mouse game of furtive glances played out for the next fifteen minutes. When Mercy figured enough long-distance foreplay had gone by, she paid for her drink and stepped away from the bar, saying to a listening Freeman, "Making contact," before removing her earpiece.

Having made her way to the nightclub's second level, Mercy now sauntered toward the VIP section, a black clutch purse in both hands. She was met a few strides later by two of Romero's men.

Dressed like their boss but with the addition of a sport jacket, both men blocked her advance with an outstretched hand. One spoke to her in Spanish before pointing in the direction from which she had come.

Understanding what he had said to her, 'This is a private party. Go back downstairs,' she feigned ignorance of the language while raising her hands and shrugging.

The man reiterated his command.

Mercy flipped Romero, who was watching from his chair, another sensual smile, like the ones she had been casually tossing him from the bar area. This time, however, she ratcheted up her performance. Locking eyes with him, she let her jaw go slack and dragged the tip of her tongue across her pursed lips.

A half smile graced his features.

Confident her message had been received, she pouted at the two human barriers then turned to leave.

Romero spoke.

Both bodyguards pivoted toward him.

Mercy strolled toward the stairs. She could hear the conversation, *Sergio, let her through,* but she played dumb and kept walking.

Sergio spun toward Mercy and said, "Señorita, regrese."

She ignored him.

He raised his voice. "Señorita?"

Mercy glanced over her shoulder.

He beckoned her with his left hand while turning sideways and extending his other arm toward Romero.

She put a hand to her chest while eyeing a smiling Nestor Romero.

He motioned for her to come before snapping his fingers at a man across the table from him. That man stood up from his chair and stepped aside.

Mercy slipped between the bodyguards and approached Romero's table.

He stood, put his left hand on her right shoulder, then directed her toward the open seat. "Por favor. Únete a mi."

She sat and crossed her legs. "Forgive me, but," she gestured, "I don't know any Spanish."

"Ah," Romero bowed an inch while touching fingertips to his chest. "Then it is I who must ask for your forgiveness, Miss..." he waited.

"Delgado. Faith Delgado."

He took her right hand and kissed it. "Such a beautiful name."

She pretended to gush over the attention.

He pinched the gold crucifix he wore. "Everyone

must have faith, sí?"

"True," she agreed, her stomach churning, as she wondered if he said that to his victims right before he shot them in the back of the head.

He reclaimed his seat and crossed his legs at the knee. "Tell me, Miss Delgado, are you—"

"Faith." She smiled. "Please."

He nodded. "As you wish." A beat. "I'm curious. Are you from Honduras? Your accent says you are not."

"No, I'm American. I'm here with my husband on a business trip."

"Marido," repeated a surprised Romero as he arched his brows at her.

She waved him off. "Don't worry. He's busy with," she fluttered a hand, "whatever it is he does."

"You do not know what business your husband is in?"

Mercy shrugged. "As long as the bank account is full, and I have access to it, I don't really care what he does." She glanced away while putting on a sad face. "All I know is he hasn't done *me* in *months*." She came back to Romero, her countenance doing an about-face. Biting her lower lip, she took in his features while lifting her top foot to graze his calf. "Buy a girl a drink?"

Romero grinned at her subtle advance. "Once again, I must ask your forgiveness. Where are my manners? What are you drinking?"

"Ranch water," she replied, knowing she needed a low-alcohol drink to keep her wits about her.

He clapped his hands at one of his men while barking out an order.

The man hurried toward the stairs.

Romero half squinted at Mercy. "You look familiar."

Mercy's heart raced. With her disguise, she was ninety percent certain he wouldn't recognize her for who she really was. Plus, over the last ten years, she had noticed her natural voice had gotten deeper. So, as part of her subterfuge, she was using her newfound contralto voice to her advantage, making sure she accentuated it whenever she spoke. Even with these deceptions, however, there was always a chance—that leftover ten percent—that he would identify her as the one who had blown up his boathouse in the Caribbean.

"Have we ever met before, Miss Delgado?"

"Faith," she replied before shaking her head. "And I don't believe so." Pressing her sternum to the edge of the table and leaning forward, the act making her breasts appear fuller, she reached across the table to rub her palm over his right hand, hoping to get him back to thinking with another part of his anatomy. "*You*," she smiled, "I would have remembered."

...

Twenty Minutes Later...

At Mercy's behest for more privacy, Romero had ordered his girls to leave the VIP area. Now the couple

        FAR FROM MERCY

sat on a leather loveseat in the darkest corner, where the fooling around had just begun.

On Romero's right, sitting on her left hip, her right thigh laying on his groin, she cupped the left side of his face with her right hand while nibbling on his right earlobe.

Romero ran his left palm up her calf and over her gladiator sandal, pausing at the buckle around her knee before slipping his hand inside her dress.

She flinched at where he had gone, a second later fabricating a low groan while playfully easing his arm away from her. Breathing heavily into his right ear, she ran fingernails over his hairy chest, painfully aware of how difficult it was to act like you were enjoying something when you really felt like vomiting.

Romero turned his head to kiss her lips.

She tipped her head back and directed him toward her neck, toward where it would be easier to wash off his filthy DNA later on.

After planting a few kisses on the right side of her neck, he pivoted his hips into her, forcing her legs apart, as he pushed her to the loveseat's arm.

Mercy gripped his upper arms and pushed back. "Wait. Stop."

He lifted his head.

Peering into his eyes, and noticing frustration in them, *He won't be denied much longer*, she glanced right to see his bodyguards close by.

"What's wrong?" asked Romero.

"Nothing. It's just that," coming back to him, she toyed with his gold chain. "It's just that," she shot another look at his bodyguards, "this isn't very private."

"Are you bashful, mi amor?"

She dialed up a shy grin.

He smiled back at her. "Very well. I'll send them away."

"No," she countered.

He cocked his head at her. "No?"

"I mean," she stammered before manufacturing a twinkle in her eye, "I have an idea. How about we *really* have some fun?"

He frowned.

She 'bench-pressed' his upper body and uncoiled her naked legs from around his waist, positive her splayed dress was giving him a tantalizing sneak peek at the black lace thong she was wearing. "Come with me," she said, taking him by the hand and pulling him off the furniture.

"Where are we going?"

Mercy hurried out of the VIP section, her high heels scuffing over the tile flooring. "To *really* have some fun, silly."

Romero's bodyguards followed.

At the staircase, she pivoted into Romero and drew close to him. "Tell them to stay," she purred.

He glimpsed his men then faced her. "Their job is to protect me. They go wherever I go."

Mercy pouted at his chest. "Are you afraid of me, afraid that I'll hurt you or something?"

He took her by the upper arms.

She lifted her gaze but kept her chin down, her wig's corkscrew-like locks playing over her eyes and cheeks, veiling most of her physical qualities.

He regarded her. "How could I be afraid of such belleza?"

Beauty, Mercy translated in her mind while the butterflies returned to her stomach, those same butterflies that always showed up right before you heaved.

He took her hand. "Lead the way, señorita Faith."

• • •

Outside, behind the nightclub, in the backseat of Freeman and Mercy's Hyundai Tucson, Mercy pulled a small, round, flat container from her clutch purse. After plucking two pills, she returned the plastic tin to her purse and gave one pill to Romero.

He studied the offering. "What's this?"

"Something to get us in the mood." She popped her tablet into her mouth then took a swig of water from a water bottle she had swiped on the way out of the nightclub. "Here." She held out the beverage.

He went from her to the pill to her again.

She tilted her head to one side. "It just gives you a

little buzz, I promise." She jiggled the bottle. "It'll make things," she ran a hand over his nearest thigh, "wild."

Following another back-and-forth, he tossed the drug into his mouth, shook his head at the water bottle, then swallowed.

Mercy dropped the container onto the seat and sat on his lap, her thighs straddling his.

He took her in his arms and moved in for a kiss.

She rocked forward while throwing her head backward, his puckered lips landing on her chest, on the fabric of her dress.

Grunting, Romero slid to his left and threw her onto the backseat to his right. Her head almost slammed against the door.

"Easy, big boy. The rough stuff will come later."

"No." Forcing his body between her legs, he crossed her arms at the wrists, wrapped a seatbelt around them, then pulled on the strap. "The rough stuff starts," using his free hand, he pried open her jaw, "now." He spit his pill into her mouth, clamped her jaw shut, and pinched her nose.

Mercy writhed. Twisting her body, flailing her legs, she dug her heels into the seat, the ceiling, the back of the front seats. She wrenched on her restraints, but they only seemed to get tighter, the edges of the material digging into her skin.

The pill she had taken was a placebo. It had been marked. But the one she had given to Romero was real, a sedative Jorge Montoya had procured from a contact of his. The dosage had been tailored for a man of Nestor Romero's weight. Not strong enough to knock him out, it would have rendered him more compliant, so Mercy and Freeman could get their prisoner to the private airport where a plane was waiting to fly the three of them to the States. How that same dosage would affect a woman of her weight was unknown.

Unable to hold off any longer, Mercy swallowed the drug, but continued the fight. She managed to pull off the acrobatic feat of bringing her right knee almost behind her ear. Planting the spike of her heel into her aggressor's chest, she drove him backward.

Romero lost his grip on the seatbelt.

She wrangled free, scooted further up the door, and kicked him in the face.

He touched the cut on his left cheek, glimpsed the blood, then smirked at her. "Enérgica, I see. I like spirited women."

"Yeah? Well, there's a lot more where that," seeing Romero's 'twin' brother appear, "where that," Mercy blinked twice, folded her right leg again, and sent her foot toward his nose. In her mind, she was thinking she was going to hit him hard enough to drive the spike out the back of his head.

With his left arm, Romero lazily deflected the strike.

Her leg flopped onto the Tucson's floorboard.

He slid closer to her.

Her world spinning now, Mercy felt her body sinking deeper into the cushion beneath her. Her face and chest were getting hotter and hotter.

Sandwiching her bent left leg between the right side of his rib cage and the backseat, Romero placed her right leg on his lap and ran a coarse palm over her thigh and down her sandal straps, before reversing course.

Unable to resist him, unable to feel him, or feel anything for that matter, she was at the mercy of a notorious cartel leader. Her eyes drooped. Her right arm flopped outward, the back of her hand slapping onto the Tucson's floormat a split-second later.

Nestor Romero half smiled at her.

She watched his smirking face blur before everything around her faded to black.

"Bienvenida de nuevo, Señorita Mercy Sands."

Mercy's head rolled right, and her body went limp, her mind translating the last words she heard. "Welcome back, Miss Mercy Sands."

Four Hours Later
Northeast of San Pedro Sula
Near the Gulf of Honduras

Mercy blinked a few more times. Fifteen minutes ago, she had opened her eyes, and been able to keep them open, for the first time since being drugged. Her initial grogginess was wearing off now, and her thoughts had been centered on deciphering who had betrayed her to Romero. Agent Walt Freeman had been the prime suspect. He had known the entire plan to nab Romero. But when the first gentle beams of dawn had started peeking through a tiny window near the ceiling of whatever cold, damp, humid room she was being held in—illuminating a man-sized lump a few feet from her—her suspicions of Walt Freeman had quickly faded.

Lying on her back, on a hard concrete floor, still in her dress and heels, Mercy shifted her gaze toward Freeman's dead body. She spied the gunshot wound at the base of his skull. His premature demise had cleared him of any wrongdoing. That is, unless he *had* been her betrayer, but was then ultimately betrayed by another betrayer. She grimaced at the rising pain behind her forehead. This was another reason she was glad she was

ALEX ANDER   83

out of this business and working at a diner. The lies, the deceit; nothing was ever as it seemed. *I'll never complain about a disgruntled customer again.*

After losing consciousness in the backseat of the Tucson, she had come to twice. The first time, she had been lying in the back of a vehicle, the darkness outside a window periodically lit up by a single light passing by. Streetlights, she had figured. The second time, two men had been hoisting her listless body by her armpits, her legs trailing, the tops of her feet dragging over rough pavement. Before passing out again, she had managed to lift her head to get a glimpse of what she knew to be Romero's Honduran villa.

Now Mercy raised a heavy right arm, flexed her fingers, then made a fist. Strength was returning, but her muscles were tight. Tired, her back stiff from laying on the hard 'bedding' beneath, she dragged a palm down her face and sighed. Physically, she felt beat up. Mentally, spiritually, she felt deflated, as if all the air had been sucked out of her lungs—like that time in sixth grade when Jennifer Winslow had landed a lucky gut punch during a schoolyard fight.

Maybe it was the aftereffects of the drug. Or maybe she was simply tired of the fight. All she wanted was to be home, at a ball game, watching her son play. Doubts crept into her psyche, doubts about her decision to take Romero at the nightclub. *Maybe I should've waited for the strike team to arrive and taken the villa by force.*

Biting her lower lip, she glanced at Freeman's body again. Perhaps her efforts to limit bloodshed had clouded her judgement. She closed her eyes. *And now a good man is dead.* She contemplated that. *Unless he was the one who, in reality, sold me out.* Then again, maybe Romero had recognized her from the start and was simply waiting to turn the tables on her, kidnap her.

With all ten fingers, Mercy rubbed her throbbing forehead before folding her hands around her nose and mouth. *Father God, I*—her chest rose high then sunk low—*I need Your help. I'm not sure what to do next.* She saw her son's face. Every muscle in her body convulsed at the thought of him becoming an orphan. She took a few deep breaths, slowly letting out each one, hoping to calm the mounting pressure, the negative thoughts, thoughts that were telling her it was too late to do anything, too late to find a way back to him.

For the next few minutes, she prayed, not really knowing what to say but knowing what she wanted—to be home in Iowa with her boy. A beat later, her thoughts turned toward a scripture passage, one she had come across early in her study of the Bible, from the Book of Micah: *Seek justice, love mercy, walk humbly with your God.*

The law enforcement side of her had taken to that passage; specifically, the part about justice. Digging deeper, she had discovered her God was a just God who wanted his children to do what was right, to love one another, and to stay close to the Father, trust the Father in all things.

Mercy interlaced her fingers atop her chest, her mind buzzing, her spirit getting a shot of energy, as she strained to hear the 'voice' inside her, the same inner awareness she had experienced many times since her faith had started growing.

Moments later, unsure if seconds or minutes had passed, she opened her eyes to stare at the ceiling. The words she had been searching for seemed to spill out of her mouth without much effort. Half thinking them and half breathing them aloud, she said under her breath, "Father, give me the strength to do Your will, the purpose for which You have called me here, brought me to this very place and time in history." Seeing Nestor Romero's face, she inwardly nodded, mindful that her knowledge of the man made her the only person qualified to bring him to justice. "Guide my every step and lead me safely back to my son. In the holy name of Your only begotten Son, our Lord and Savior, Jesus Christ, I pray. Amen."

Mercy rolled onto her belly and pushed herself to her feet, her entire being feeling alive, confident once more. After a quick pass around her 'cell,' she tried the knob on the only door in the room. It was locked. She peered out the window—a window too small to pass a loaf of bread through—and saw blades of grass along with tall weeds. *Must be in the basement.* She knew the guards would soon come to take her. To what end, she didn't know, but she

 FAR FROM MERCY

knew Romero, though. And whatever he had planned for her, especially after the Caribbean incident, wasn't going to be pretty.

She stooped to search Freeman's body, finding nothing. His murderers had taken everything from his pockets, only leaving him with the clothes on his back and the shoes on his feet. Mercy eyed the leather belt around the dead man's waist, her mind recalling the seemingly heavy belt buckle attached to it. She envisioned herself swinging it, using the weighted end as a weapon against the first man to step into the room.

After rolling Freeman's corpse onto its backside, she undid the buckle and pulled.

Click.

She stopped pulling when the buckle seemed to come apart in her hands. *What the...* A moment later, she half grinned. *God bless you, Walt Freeman. May God bless you and keep you in His peace.* She then yanked the belt free of the pants it had once held up.

...

Fifteen Minutes Later...

The knob turned on the door. The door swung open. Two dark-skinned Latin American men entered the room. Both stopped just inside the doorway. One snickered as he backhanded the other man in the stomach before pointing at Mercy and saying, in Spanish,

"I bet she's praying Nestor will give her a quick death."

Having positioned herself so the window was behind her, so the sun's rays partly obscured her from whoever entered the room, Mercy was kneeling with her chin on her chest and her folded hands near her belly button, near Walt Freeman's belt buckle, which was attached to the dead man's belt that now encircled her waist. *If it be Your will, Lord*, she prayed.

Mercy had spent the last ten minutes praying, her mind conjuring the horrible things she would most likely have to do, terrible acts like those she had worked so hard to forget. Now they were back, though, provoked by the evil lurking only a few feet away from her. But if she wanted to apprehend Romero, escape this dark place, and make it safely back to Iowa, to her son, then so be it. She had reconciled her fate with her faith. And in the end, she knew her God would have the ultimate say, and she was trusting in His goodness and guidance. Psalm 23 came to her, and she inwardly recited the verse. *I will fear no evil, for you are with me; your rod and your staff comfort me.*

Still smirking, the men approached her.

She glimpsed them then closed her eyes again. *Forgive me, my Lord...*

The men bent over, both reaching down to grab her by the arms.

Mercy squeezed the buckle — 'Click.'

Two curved pieces jutted out from the clasp's sides,

at nine and three o'clock.

...for what I must do. She yanked out those pieces then thrust her arms upward, plunging into flesh the push daggers she clutched in her fists.

Earlier, before the men had arrived, Mercy had used one of the push daggers to slice away the lower third of her dress before cutting a knee-to-waist slit up the right side for freedom of movement. Now she jumped up, onto her bare feet.

Unsure of what had just happened to them, both Latin American men stood in place, each clasping his throat with both hands.

Mercy let loose with a wild flurry of punches to her captors' face and neck area. She connected with multiple jabs, and left and right crosses, the push daggers' two-inch triangular blades puncturing skin on the way in, then shredding muscle on the way out.

Backing away, while trying to keep blood from spilling from their necks, the men were successful at deflecting some of the incoming blows, but the push daggers still mangled their wrists and forearms.

Bending at the knees, Mercy stepped left and came up with a right uppercut, driving a push dagger deep into one man's Adam's apple.

His body went limp.

She spun right and backhanded the other guy with her right fist, slicing the blade across his throat, before thrusting her left push dagger into his Adam's apple.

The men collapsed to the floor, twitching, choking

on their own blood.

Mercy let her arms fall to her sides as she hung her head. Knife fights were brutal. Few died quickly. But she had done her best to make their deaths as quick and painless as possible. She closed her eyes. *Have mercy on their souls, Lord. I don't know their pasts, their faith in You and Your Son.* The gurgling noises faded. *But You do. And if it be Your will, forgive them of their sins.*

By the time her intercessory prayer was over, the men were dead.

Mercy cleaned the push daggers, reinserted them into the buckle around her waist, then searched the corpses. She found no weapons, nothing that could assist her with her mission. *Seems Romero's gotten smarter since our last encounter.*

Stepping through the doorway to see a set of wooden stairs in the middle of a room not much bigger than the one she had just left, she frowned. *This isn't the basement that I remember.*

Mercy took the stairs to the next level, where outdoor power equipment and gardening tools filled the space, double doors across from her. She snaked between a lawn tractor and a push mower to a partially open side door.

After poking her head outside and seeing a rising sun's rays peeping through trees, on her right, to bathe Romero's villa in the distance, on her left, she scanned the immediate area then darted toward a massive tree, a

Kapok tree, on the edge of a nearby forest. The hundred-foot-plus tall specimen's buttress roots were high enough to conceal a full-grown man. Mercy slipped between two roots and glanced back at the building she had exited, now recognizing it for what it was—a storage shed, albeit with the added feature of a secret, underground prison.

Mercy confirmed no one was behind her before she pivoted right to peer over the top of a tree root to study the back side of the villa. Everything appeared quiet, much like one would expect at the dawning of a new day. She reached up and slapped the left side of her neck before spying the mashed remains of some insect. Behind her, many of the bug's relatives, along with a couple birds she didn't recognize, were humming and squawking. Already, at this early hour, the air was thick and humid.

She went back to scrutinizing the three-story, flat-roofed redbrick house with six-foot-wide balconies outside every room on the second and third levels, four on each level. Unless major renovations had been done in the last ten years, Mercy knew the interior layout, including the location of Romero's bedroom—second story, second balcony from the left—which is where he would most likely be at this time.

A solo assault, overt or covert, that involved clearing the first two floors would be extremely risky, especially if all she had were two push daggers. Sure, she could pick up weapons, hopefully a pistol, from those she killed along the way, but there was no guarantee her next victim would have a gun. Plus, once the gun went off, the gunshot would draw in every henchman in the house. No. She needed to find a silent way into Romero's bedroom.

Mercy cocked her head at the backside of the villa, her eyes taking in every angle, ledge, and lip she could make out, before settling on a black drainage pipe that ran from the rooftop to the ground on the right side of the structure. She spied Romero's balcony then slowly panned right, back to the drainpipe. Envisioning her bare feet, she grimaced. *Never done it barefooted before, but,* she thought, *but it just might work.*

The back door opened, and a man emerged from the villa, his path taking him straight for the storage shed.

Mercy put her back to the tree trunk and waited.

About her height, his hair long and shiny in the sunlight, the dark-skinned Latin American man ducked into the storage shed via the open side door.

She heard him bark out a question in Spanish, asking what was taking so long. Her heart pounded in her chest. Once he discovered his fallen compadres, and saw that their prisoner had escaped, her element of surprise was gone.

Mercy sneaked back into the shed to see him standing at the top of the stairs, his back to her.

He shouted down the staircase again.

Crouching, she weaved her way back around the push mower and lawn tractor. Having released her push daggers when she was outside, she now clenched one in each hand as she crept up behind him.

Shaking his head, he cursed while taking the first step.

Staying on the balls of her feet, Mercy darted forward and lifted her right leg to plant her foot in the center of his back.

Startled, he whipped his head to his left, his torso twisting as well.

Her foot glanced across his right shoulder blade, and she lost her balance.

The Latin American was in between downward steps, and the glancing blow was enough to make him stumble. With no handrail, he tumbled down the steps.

Falling, and nearly doing the splits, Mercy followed him, skidding headfirst down the treads before rolling onto her left shoulder. She let go of her right push dagger to hook the backside of a step with her fingers. Her legs kept going, and her feet smacked down onto the floor. A jolt of pain ran up the back of her right leg.

Latin American got to his feet and went for the pistol on his right hip.

Still clutching the push dagger in her left hand, Mercy shoved herself away from the staircase, charged forward, and slashed downward, eleven o'clock to five o'clock, across his right wrist.

'LA' grabbed his injury.

The pistol banged off the concrete.

She reversed course and swiped her left fist across his

face.

The two-inch blade filleted his left cheek in half while opening a one-inch gash at the right corner of his mouth.

He clutched his face with his left hand then threw out his right fist, catching Mercy in the center of her forehead.

Her head rocking backward, and her left foot slipping, she fell onto her left butt cheek.

LA went for his gun.

She swung her right leg across her body and kicked the weapon into the corner to her left.

He chased it.

Mercy rolled onto her belly and caught his trailing foot.

Face first, he sprawled onto the floor, but immediately scrambled a few feet and stretched out his right arm.

Jumping to her feet...

LA's open right hand came down onto the gun.

...Mercy lunged forward and landed on top of him.

His fingers closed around the grip, and he twisted his body clockwise.

Driving her right forearm into the back of his neck, she crawled up his back, swung her left arm over her head, and jammed the push dagger into his right wrist, the tip of the blade punching all the way through and taking a chunk out of the floor.

            FAR FROM MERCY

LA bellowed.

Mercy rocked backward onto her haunches, grasped his long, greasy hair in both hands, and banged his head against the concrete. The first blow sounded like a shopper testing a watermelon for freshness. The second whack was like a sledgehammer coming down onto a four-by-four post that had already been sunk four feet into the ground.

LA stopped yelling and writhing, his body going flaccid.

Mercy put her bloody right palm down and leaned over her adversary, her lungs demanding oxygen. She wiped her left forearm across her forehead and down her face, clearing away sweat. A moment later, she trundled off LA and flopped onto her back. Her chest heaved a few times as she filled her lungs with stale air.

She lifted her right knee then reached around to massage the back of her leg, to rub out the stinger she had gotten when her heel had slammed onto the floor earlier. Eyeing her motionless opponent, knowing he was still alive, she stripped off his shoes and socks. After stuffing his mouth with the socks, she used the shoelaces to bind his wrists and ankles.

With him now neutralized and unable to cry out for help, she searched him. Her haul was a loaded Taurus TH45 pistol, and a spare magazine topped off with thirteen 45 ACP cartridges.

Mercy confiscated the weapon, as well as a leather,

outside-the-waistband holster—with an attached mag carrier forward of the gun—then threaded Freeman's belt through the OWB holster's slots. With the rig now secured around her waist, and the push daggers back inside the buckle, she headed upstairs.

With the sun rising and the temperatures only getting hotter, Mercy had little time before the villa, and the surrounding grounds, came alive with activity. After leaving the storage shed, she had stayed close to a tree line while sneaking up to the back of the house. Now she crouched at the base of the structure beside the black drainpipe she had spotted earlier.

After rubbing the back of her right leg, hoping to keep the muscle she had tweaked earlier loose, she lifted her left leg, pushed off a metal generator enclosure, and got a right foothold on the nearest drainpipe joint while further up cupping the pipe with her hands.

Years ago, when Mercy was in her late teens, she had dated a guy who was big into parkour. Amazed at how he could transform urban objects, objects that most people would see as obstacles, into toeholds and finger grips, she had trained with him. And while she had never attained his level of skill, she had become fairly adept at parkour's various elements—climbing, vaulting, swinging, among others. One difference from then and now, however, was that back then she had worn shoes. Plus, she was almost twenty years younger then, too.

With her palms and soles squeezing round metal, Mercy pulled and pushed herself up to the next pipe joint. With her feet on the joint's lip, her knees pressing on the rough brick, and her butt hanging just below her feet, she estimated the distance between her and the second-floor balcony on her eleven o'clock. A fall from this height wouldn't be that dangerous. But the noise from the fall would probably draw a few eyeballs, and plenty of guns, too.

After taking a breath and exhaling, she straightened her legs while repeatedly letting go of the pipe and getting a higher hold. Having shimmied to almost even with the balcony's floor, her thigh muscles shaking and burning, she pushed off to her left while stretching out her arms.

Mercy's fingers caught the trim on the balcony as her legs swung underneath. With her sleeveless, royal-blue, knee-length dress waving, as her legs swung back again, she used the momentum, while pulling with her arms, to catapult herself higher and get a stronger hold on two of the terrace handrail's vertical metal stiles. She then raised her left leg, got a foothold, then climbed onto the manmade overhang.

Once she was on top of the handrail, she leaped into the air while throwing her arms upward. Wincing at a sharp pain, instinctively reaching for the source of her discomfort, her right hamstring, Mercy gripped a stile with her left hand, as her legs whipped out to her left, straining the muscles down the right side of her body. Gritting her teeth and still grimacing, she was prepping to slingshot herself back up, to grab on with her right hand, when someone stepped out from the room above her.

Hanging by one arm, Mercy pivoted left, got her right fingernails around the square head of a lateral bolt beneath the terrace, and waited, knowing if this person peeked over the railing, or noticed her fingers coiled around the stile, or if another person stepped out from the room below, her surprise attack would be over.

A yawn came from above, followed by a feminine sigh. A minute later, another person, a man, came out of the same room. In Spanish, he implored the woman to come back to bed.

Something crawled onto Mercy's right hand.

Flinching, she relaxed her grip before squeezing again. She tilted her head backward to squint at the shadows hiding her hand, shadows that were also home to whatever creature that had been displaced by her arrival.

When her eyes couldn't make out what was on her hand, Mercy's mind took over, as she imagined a big, hairy tarantula, or one of many spiders inhabiting Honduras. If there were ever a time in her life when she had wanted to 'scream like a little girl,' this was it.

With the couple above her playing 'slap and tickle,'

Mercy felt the creepy-crawly thing slink over her wrist and down her forearm, coming into the light a moment later. She let out an inward sigh when she saw it was a light-brown salamander. While still gross in her estimation, it was not as bad as what she had envisioned, especially for someone like her, who harbored a lifelong fear of spiders.

The Spanish-speaking woman giggled as the couple ducked back into their room, the sliding door closing a beat later.

Mercy let go of the bolt, shook the salamander from her arm, then contorted her body to grab a stile with her right hand.

Seconds later, perched atop the third-floor veranda's handrail, she jumped up, careful not to rely too heavily on her right leg. She curled her fingers over the edge of the flat roof, pulled, swung her left leg over, then rolled onto the surface.

Getting to her feet, she made a face and clenched her glutes before slipping a forefinger under her dress and under the 'thong' of her thong, near her tailbone, to extract the foreign object. "Whew," she sighed, pushing the lingerie to her ankles. *Wish I had done that before I started climbing.* She stepped out of the skimpy garment then limped down the roofline while kneading her stinging muscles at the back of her right thigh.

Once she was in line with Romero's second-floor balcony, the traceuse traced a reverse path back down.

Slithering over the edge of the roof, Mercy dropped onto the third-floor terrace's handrail, hopped down to the floor, outside the railing, then jumped off backward and grabbed the stiles where they met the floor.

Following a forward and backward swing of her legs, she let go. Her bare feet landed on the railing outside Romero's bedroom before she stepped off and silently touched down onto the carpeted surface.

Mercy drew her Taurus TH45. Her gait hitching with every other step, she sneaked up to the open sliding door and put her back to the redbrick, the sliding door on her right. After glancing around, as well as down toward the lower verandas, verifying no one had seen her, she pointed her pistol toward the curtains fluttering in the doorway and slipped into the room.

     FAR FROM MERCY

The room was brightening, so it didn't take long for Mercy's eyes to adjust, as she crept toward a king-sized bed on the other side of the room, bypassing a wooden armoire, two straight-back chairs, and an ornate floor lamp, her bare feet sinking into a soft Persian rug. Droning in a corner by itself, an oscillating floor fan made a pass, displacing her wig's curly hair around her shoulders, while making the perspiration on her face and arms feel like an ice pack.

On the bed, Nestor Romero lay with a sheet up to his nipples, thick tufts of black hair swirling around them. To his left, a young girl lay on her right side, the same bedsheet pulled up to her neck, her long dark hair draped over her bare left shoulder and arm.

Mercy squinted at the girl. In this light, she couldn't be sure, but judging by her childlike features, the girl was far from adulthood. Mercy gritted her teeth, partly due to instinct, at wanting to shoot Romero between the eyes, and partly to help disperse those same murderous inclinations.

Approaching from Romero's side of the bed, Mercy barely touched the muzzle of the TH45 to the man's forehead and gradually applied pressure, stopping right before the slide began to retract.

Blinking a few times, he lazily tried to brush aside the

gun.

Mercy slapped at his hand.

His eyes opening fully, they went from the gun to the woman holding the gun.

"Nestor Romero," said the former ICE agent, "you're under arrest for," she paused, her mind coming up with too many crimes to list, "for a lot of stuff."

Awake now, he smiled at her, his upper lip folding at a sinister, crooked angle. "I thought you had left the agency, Ms. Sands."

She shrugged a shoulder. "One last hurrah, I guess."

The girl stirred, raising an arm to stretch.

Romero went from the girl to Mercy.

Mercy could see his ill intentions. "While I prefer to take you in alive, I'm good with just killing you outright. So, don't get any ideas."

The prone girl opened her eyes, her face stricken with terror at what she was seeing.

Mercy backed up and waved the gun toward the floor, her focus squarely on Romero. "On the floor."

He flung the sheet off to show a pair of black silk boxers before swinging his hairy legs over the side of the mattress, standing, then going to his knees.

"*All* the way down," she said. "Kiss the rug."

He chuckled, "Funny," before glancing back at the girl on the bed, "I think I said the same thing last night."

Gripping the Taurus tighter, Mercy fought the urge to end this here and now.

"The rug thing is good, though, too." He got down on his belly. "I'll have to remember that one."

She regarded the young girl cowering at the headboard, holding the sheet up to her neck. "Don't be afraid, sweetie. I won't hurt you."

The girl frowned.

Mercy repeated what she had said, in Spanish, before noticing the girl relax a bit. "¿Cómo te llamas?"

"Dacia," replied the girl.

Mercy eyed Dacia's thin arms and small stature. "¿Cuántos años tienes, Dacia?"

"Quince."

Mercy barely shook her head, *Fifteen*, before glaring down at Romero, her homicidal tendencies from years ago threatening to overtake her newfound faith in Jesus Christ. *My Lord, please don't let me stumble.* She faced Dacia. "¿Por qué estás aquí," she gestured toward Romero, "con él?"

Dacia brought her knees to her chest to hug her legs. A second later, turning sullen, she laid her left cheek on her kneecaps. "Mis padres fueron asesinados. No me queda familia."

Mercy's heart broke at the girl's story, a story she had become familiar with during her time among the gang lords and human traffickers. Dacia's parents had been killed, and the girl had no family left to care for her. Mercy didn't want to ask what the girl had been forced to do to survive. She was just glad she had met this poor thing before Romero tired of her and sold her off as a sex slave. She smiled at Dacia. "¿Te gustaría volver a los Estados Unidos conmigo?"

Dacia's eyes got bigger. "America?"

Mercy nodded. She didn't know if she could legally pull it off, but with millions upon millions of people flooding the U.S. southern border illegally, most of them military-aged men claiming political asylum, if ever there was a true case of someone in need of help from the United States, this orphaned kid was it. "Sí, America," she replied.

The girl looked toward Romero then came back to the woman offering her a way out of her predicament.

Mercy read the girl's mind. "No te preocupes por él. He's going to prison."

"This is all quite touching, Ms. Sands, but aren't you forgetting something?" Romero waited. "You won't get out of here alive. My men will gun you down the first chance they get."

"Well, if they do," she countered, while looking around for something she could use to bind his hands, "then the last person I'll be sure to kill is *you*." She kicked his left foot. "Now spread your legs and don't move."

He snickered into the carpeting. "Again, I believe I said those very same words las—"

Mercy slammed the two-pound pistol into his left kidney. It was a knee-jerk reaction, and she instantly regretted it, regretted having allowed him to goad her into doing something not in line with her character. *Forgive me, Lord.*

Contorting his body from the blow, the cartel leader grunted, then laughed in between coughs.

•••

Minutes Later...

While Dacia had gotten dressed, Mercy had yanked a white belt from a robe draped over a chair, tied a slip knot at one end, then cinched that end around Romero's neck. She then bound his wrists at the middle of his back with the other end. With his hands at this height, if he tried to escape or fight back, his struggles would only tighten the noose around his neck.

Now spotting a cell phone on the nightstand next to Romero's side of the bed, Mercy tossed it to Dacia, telling her to stuff it into her jeans. The trio then left the bedroom. Wearing only his boxers, Romero led the way with Mercy directly behind him, her left hand firmly gripping the belt up by his shoulder blades, her right hand pointing the Taurus TH45 at his spine, just north of his tailbone. If she pressed the trigger, he would drop immediately.

Having already been instructed to keep an eye on their 'six,' Dacia was a half-step behind Mercy.

Outside the room, in a hallway-slash-terrace that overlooked the main floor, Mercy nudged Romero with her left fist. "Slow and easy," she said while casting alternating glances from the hallway ahead to the wooden handrail on her left and the first floor below.

From somewhere in the house, the distant high-pitched whirr of an overtaxed motor was coupled with what sounded like a constant barrage of pebbles striking a windowpane.

"One shot from one of my men, and you're dead," said Romero. "And this is all over."

They passed two closed doors on the right before coming up on a staircase on the left.

"And you'll have no idea where that shot will come from," he added.

Mercy pushed him.

Lifting his bare left foot, he took the first tread. "Will it come from behind?" He carefully descended the steps. "Will it come from around a corner on your—"

She tugged on the belt.

He stiffened as his windpipe compressed.

"Shut...Up," she said.

He smiled. "Just making conversation," he said, his voice strained.

She motioned for him to get going again.

Dacia slid her left hand down the railing while staring toward the upstairs hallway, watching to see if any of the doors opened.

Halfway down the stairs, a man in khaki pants and a white pullover rounded a corner and strolled toward the threesome. He saw the scene, drew his pistol, and pointed it in the direction of his boss.

Mercy pulled on the belt while driving the gun into Romero's backside. "Tell him to drop it."

Romero said nothing.

"Do it," she said.

A moment later, Romero twisted his neck then spoke in Spanish.

The employee laid his pistol on the floor.

Staring at the gunman, Mercy jerked her head to the side and said, "Patéalo y acuéstate en el suelo."

The man kicked the pistol away then laid down on the floor.

"Mercy," shouted Dacia, pointing toward the upstairs. "¡Allí arriba!"

Mercy pulled Romero closer while twisting her upper body to the left and pointing the Taurus upward.

Behind the upstairs railing, a half-dressed man aimed a gun at her. He fired.

The bullet whizzed by her left ear.

A coiled lock from her wig landed on her left shoulder then drifted toward the stairs.

Mercy returned fire.

Covering her ears, Dacia spun away from the firearm's booming report.

A 45ACP bullet struck Mercy's target above his sternum and below his throat.

He wobbled in place then folded over the railing. His

legs followed a second later, and he crashed onto a glass coffee table, shattering the furniture into a million pieces.

The man on the floor scrambled to his feet and ran for his gun, the one he had kicked away earlier.

Mercy swung her firearm clockwise and got off two quick shots.

One bullet hit him in the left shoulder. The other round-nosed, full metal jacketed bullet pierced his rib cage and heart.

Grabbing his wound, he toppled to the floor and slid three feet, leaving a red skid mark behind him.

Mercy shoved Romero. "Go!" She glanced behind her to see Dacia still cowering. "Dacia, ¡vamos! ¡vamos!"

The girl stood. Wild-eyed, she took in the carnage, then quickly closed the distance between her and her protector.

Knowing there would be transportation parked in a circular driveway out front, but also aware that the territory between the cars and her was a highly trafficked route, Mercy steered Romero toward the kitchen at the back of the villa.

The now deafening 'motor and pebbles' noise wound down before stopping altogether.

Entering the kitchen, the group happened upon two men. One was sitting on a stool at a small table, a fork in his hand, his back to her, while another was scanning the inside of a refrigerator.

The seated man cranked his head toward the interruption.

Mercy sidestepped right and brought the full weight of the Taurus down against his right temple.

Knocked unconscious, he fell face first into his scrambled eggs before his body slithered off the stool, his chin dragging the plate off the table.

Yellow and white pieces rained down on top of him.

'Refrigerator Man' spun around, the mixing cup from a blender in his right hand.

Resting the TH45 on Romero's left shoulder, Mercy had a clear shot at RM. But when she saw his baby-faced features, she eased off the gun's trigger. *He can't be over sixteen.* She recalled the teen she had gunned down in the Caribbean. He, too, had been under eighteen. Back then, she had figured if you were old enough to carry a gun, then you were old enough to die. The new Mercy, however, had a hard time acting on that motto.

Guiding Romero forward, she shook her head at RM. "No lo hagas."

His eyes as big as saucers, gaping at the gun aimed his way, RM dropped the container, his green breakfast slurry spilling onto the floor. A tick later, he drew his gun.

"No," commanded Mercy.

He froze. His stainless-steel revolver had cleared the holster but was pointing at the floor.

She shook her head again. "No. Déjalo caer." She

waited, her heart in her throat. *Please, just drop it.*

RM licked his lips, peeked at the gun, then came back to her.

"Déjalo caer," she repeated.

After giving Romero a quick look, RM slowly squatted to lay his weapon on the green goo ahead of his feet before rising with his hands in the air.

Mercy manhandled Romero past the scared teen while keeping the TH45 pointed at RM. She jerked her head in the direction from which the trio had come. "Ir. Sal de aquí."

The kid took a few steps to his right, glimpsed Dacia, turned his back on Mercy, then bolted out of the kitchen.

Mercy glimpsed Dacia before motioning toward the discarded gun. "Coge el arma."

Dacia picked up the six-shot, snub-nosed Taurus 856 and held it out to Mercy.

Knowing the gun would be simple to operate, Mercy dipped her forehead toward the girl. "Quédatelo. Puede que lo necesites."

Dacia examined the revolver then eyed Mercy. "No sé nada sobre armas."

Mercy couldn't believe she was about to say what she had heard many times in the movies. *Point and shoot.* "Simplemente apunta el arma y aprieta el gatillo."

Dacia gave the 856 another look, nodded, then gripped the gun in her left hand.

After instructing the girl on where to keep the

revolver pointed, specifically, not at her, Mercy then pushed Romero out a side door and into the side yard. Off to her right, she saw the back half of a black SUV parked in the circular driveway. Over her shoulder, she heard excited back-and-forth exchanges coming from inside the house. The gunshots had awakened everyone, and they were discovering the dead bodies.

• • •

After checking the first two vehicles and not seeing keys in the ignition, Mercy now saw that the same wasn't true for the Hyundai Tucson Mercy and the late Walt Freeman had used. She opened the tailgate, stuffed Romero into the cargo area, then eased the tailgate shut with a satisfying click of the locking mechanism. She ordered Dacia to get into the backseat while withdrawing the push daggers from her belt buckle.

A minute later, having flattened two tires on each of the other four vehicles parked around the circular driveway, finishing with the lead vehicle, Mercy now ran back toward the third-in-line Tucson, the villa on her nine o'clock. On her right, in the middle of a round patch of well-manicured green grass, a stone sculpture of an ancient Roman soldier, in full battle gear, spewed water into a clamshell-shaped bowl.

A shout came from the villa's front porch.

With her escape so near, Mercy didn't have the

luxury to verify the threat. She drew her Taurus TH45 and fired toward the doorway. Return fire sent her to a crouch behind the car ahead of the Tucson.

More gunshots.

Bullets pinged off metal above her head, one of them continuing on to take the left ear off the 'Roman soldier.'

She laid on her right shoulder and acquired her target from between the black asphalt and the bottom of the car she was using for cover. She worked the Taurus' trigger twice.

Using a white Roman-style column for cover, her would-be killer clutched his left shoulder and spun counterclockwise, away from the pillar.

Mercy hopped to her feet and shot out of her stance. A zap from her right leg doubled her over, sending her to her right knee as she reached back to cup her hamstring. *Not now. Not now.* Rising, hobbling forward, she scrambled behind the wheel of the Hyundai and tossed her gun onto the passenger seat. She started the SUV, ran the gearshift, and stomped on the gas pedal, her fingers lowering the passenger window as she whirled the wheel to the left.

The Tucson lurched ahead.

Navigating the rounded driveway, bypassing parked cars on her three o'clock, she picked up the Taurus, aimed it out the passenger window, and let loose with a double-tap.

Both shots hit the man she had winged earlier, square

in the chest.

Coming to the straightaway portion of the drive, she let her right foot get heavy on the accelerator. Seconds later, she mashed the brake pedal while cranking the wheel to the left.

The SUV took the turn on 'two wheels.'

She wrenched the steering wheel back to the right then slid her foot from the 'brake' to the 'gas.'

The Hyundai Tucson zoomed away from the villa with the villa's owner tied up and bouncing around in the vehicle's cargo area.

Mercy peeled off her black, curly, lace front wig, as well as the wig grip underneath, and tossed them both onto the front passenger seat. She then undid her low bun. After a quick scalp massage, a couple shakes of her head, and some finger-combing, her long, naturally blonde hair was back in place.

"I give you credit," said Romero. "If I hadn't known what you'd be wearing, I would've never recognized you."

Mercy glimpsed his reflection in the rearview mirror. He was sitting up in the cargo area, leaning back, where the tailgate met the right-rear corner.

Sitting on her left butt cheek in the backseat, Dacia kept her Taurus revolver trained on his chest.

"The years have been good to you," continued Romero. "You were gorgeous in that dress at the nightclub. And those heels you had on," he let out a low whistle, "classy *and* sexy."

Mercy faced forward, determined not to let him get under her skin.

"You really set me back when you escaped my place in the Caribbean, you know that?" He shook his head once. "I had five million dollars of coke stashed all throughout that boat you blew up. It was supposed to be delivered the next day." He glanced out a window. "Plus, the buyer had already paid *half* up front." He spied the back of her head. "As I'm sure you can well imagine, he wasn't too happy with me."

Mercy let him babble as she thought about his first words to her. *If I hadn't known what you'd be wearing, I would've never recognized you.* The only person who knew what she would be wearing to the nightclub was Walt Freeman. But if he had been her betrayer, then why was he lying on the floor beneath the tool shed with a bullet in the back of his head? She squeezed her eyes shut then blinked a few times. *Something's not adding up.* Outside of Jorge Montoya, no one else knew about her plan to take Romero at the club. She barely shook her head. *Jorge would never sell me out.* In the next instant, she cocked her head while squinting at Romero's reflection again. *Unless someone was threatening his family.* If that were true, then would the plane she was expecting from Montoya be waiting for her at the airstrip?

•••

Forty Minutes Later...
Having navigated the Hyundai down a tree-lined path, and now driving into a clearing, Mercy was relieved to learn her friend Montoya was not her betrayer, as she

eyed a blue-and-white Cessna Caravan parked at the
start of a grassy runway.

Surrounded by forests, this private airstrip was not
well known. In the past, it had been used by drug cartels
to move illegal narcotics out of the country. But that had
stopped thirty years ago when the cartel leaders had
upgraded to a new location fifty miles to the southeast,
closer to where their product was being grown.

Mercy slowed, her eyes taking in the tree line. Her
initial relief had been replaced with a healthy dose of
suspicion. While she had not expected to meet Montoya
here, she was at least expecting to meet a pilot. But where
was the pilot's car? Did someone drop him off and leave?
She spied the single-engine turboprop. *Maybe he's getting
some sleep inside.* After all, Mercy was several hours
overdue from the timeframe she had given Montoya.

The Tucson rolled to a stop fifty feet from the
Cessna's tail section, on the aircraft's five o'clock.

Mercy ran the gearshift to 'Park,' sat back in her seat,
and gave the woods another long look. The rising sun
hadn't cleared the treetops, so the surrounding land was
sort of in the shadows. Beyond the tree line, however,
everything was dark. She drew her Taurus, exchanged the
partial mag for the full one, then shoved the 'partial' into
her belt before holstering the TH45. She told Dacia to
stay put then stepped out of the vehicle.

All around her, early morning insects were buzzing,
their loud noises creating a constant hum that seemed to

drown out every other noise.

She reached up and wiped her moist brow, the sweat there a result of both having left the SUV's cool, climate-controlled interior and the anxiety welling up inside her. She made her way to the rear of the vehicle, her head on a swivel, and opened the tailgate.

"You seem nervous, Mercy. Something wrong," asked Romero, a smirk on his face as he tipped his head from side to side before twisting his neck.

"Get out," she barked, before motioning for Dacia to do the same thing.

He swung his legs out, scooted forward, then stood.

Mercy closed the tailgate.

Romero rolled his shoulders then loosened his back muscles.

"Let's go." She drew her Taurus, grabbed the belt at the middle of his back, and directed him toward the Caravan, her pistol aimed at his spine again, her eyes scanning left and right.

Holding her revolver in her left hand, Dacia fell in beside Mercy, and the trio walked toward the plane.

Halfway there, two gunshots rang out.

Dacia arched her back and spun to the ground while gripping her left arm.

Flinching, Mercy crouched, her head and pistol pivoting toward where the reports had come from, her nine o'clock.

Romero swung his right leg backward, kicking his

captor in the shin, before breaking her hold on him and running toward where the gunshots had come from.

More bullets threw grass and dirt into the air around Mercy, as she dragged a whimpering Dacia behind the Tucson's right-front tire.

The girl took her hand away from her left upper arm.

Squatting, Mercy saw blood but no bullet holes. She pushed Dacia's palm against the cut. "It's only a flesh wound. Estas bien." Mercy peeked over the SUV to see Romero making a run for the woods. She crept to the vehicle's corner, laid her hands on the bumper, and lined up the TH45's sights. A tick later, she squeezed off a shot.

The fleeing cartel leader's gait hitched before he crumpled to the ground on the plane's seven o'clock. Hollering, he trundled back and forth, struggling to reach for the back of his right leg, his efforts impeded by the belt tightening around his neck.

A man emerged from the woods, heading straight for Romero, firing a long gun at the Hyundai as he ran.

With bullets punching holes in the SUV's sheet metal, Mercy took aim and got off several controlled shots.

The second one hit the man in the arm, but he kept going.

The fourth shot caught him in the upper chest, and he fell to his knees before skidding face first along the grass.

More incoming rounds from the tree line sent Mercy

to her butt, where she consoled a crying Dacia, telling the teen she would be okay. She eyed the plane, knowing she couldn't let a stray round ruin her escape plan. Taking another moment to assess her situation, she came up with a strategy.

Mercy opened the right-rear door and helped Dacia into the Hyundai, instructing her to keep her head down. Climbing in through the front passenger door, she wiggled over the center console and dropped into the driver's seat. Shifting the vehicle into 'Drive,' she stepped on the gas while veering left.

The Tucson's rear tires threw dirt and debris.

Fifty feet later, she made a right-ninety and jammed her foot onto the brake pedal.

The SUV skidded to a halt between a groaning Romero and the tree line from where the rounds were coming.

Mercy scrambled out the passenger door and put her gun's muzzle to the man's head. "Call them off, or you're dead." She pulled on the belt around his neck. "You hear me?"

Coughing, he continued to roll back and forth on the ground. "My leg," he grunted.

"Tell them to drop their guns and come out with their hands up. And I'll stop the bleeding." She peeked over the hood then ducked down again. "You're bleeding out, Romero. If this gunfight goes on much longer, you'll die. Is that what you want...to die on some dirty runway in the middle of—"

"Okay, okay," he said before tipping his head backward to see the trees. "Este es Néstor Romero. Deja de disparar y sal con las manos en alto. Sin armas," he added before rolling onto his left shoulder.

Seconds later, two men shuffled out of the woods. Each one still held a short-barreled rifle.

"Suelten las armas," shouted Mercy.

They tossed their weapons.

She told them to take off their clothes.

With a headshake, they refused.

She looked back at Romero. "Tell them to do it."

He ordered them to obey her.

After the men had removed their shirts, one man tossed a pistol he had hidden in the waistband at the back of his jeans.

Mercy sneered. *That's just what I thought.*

Both men stripped down to their underwear.

"Comienza a caminar por la pista. No te detengas y mantén las manos en el aire," she shouted.

The men started walking down the runway, in the direction the plane's nose was facing, their hands still up in the air.

"I did my part," said Romero. "Now," he grimaced, "stop the bleeding. Stop the bleeding."

Mercy and Dacia got the man on his feet and helped him shuffle to the Cessna, where everyone noticed a man lying on the floor at the back of the plane. The floor around the man was stained red. Mercy made a face, her mind telling her this was the pilot who was to fly them out of the country.

She rolled Romero into the plane, through the cargo door on the left side, then told Dacia to get in, and to holler if the men outside doubled back.

After dragging the deceased pilot outside—no good could come from having a dead body in the plane when she landed in Florida—she said a prayer for the man's soul then closed the cargo door, vowing to contact Montoya to ensure the dead man had a proper burial. She made a quick pass around the Cessna, doing a hasty safety inspection, before climbing the stairs to the cockpit, pulling the stairs up, and closing the door.

"Hey, what about me?" Romero cried out from his place on the floor. "You promised you'd take care of my wound."

"When we're airborne," she shot back before telling Dacia to put pressure on his leg to shut him up.

Donning a pair of earmuffs, Mercy looked at the controls. Two decades ago, she had learned to fly on her dad's Cessna Caravan. While those avionics had been before the aircraft's glass cockpit upgrade, she was still able to identify everything she needed to get this thing in the air.

Under the stressful and less-than-ideal circumstances, she conducted as much of a pre-flight checklist as she could before starting the engine. Glancing over her right

     FAR FROM MERCY

shoulder, she got Dacia's attention and motioned. "Toma asiento y abróchate el cinturón."

The teen claimed a seat and put on her seatbelt.

Seconds later, the Cessna was speeding down the airstrip.

Out of the corner of her left eye, Mercy spotted the two men she had ordered to walk away, as she pulled back on the yoke and gave the aircraft some right rudder to counteract its left turning tendencies.

The turboprop plane lifted off the ground, cleared the treetops, and rose higher and higher into the air.

The Next Day
20 July—6:36 P.M.
Washington, D.C.

One mile south of the White House, tucked away in the middle of the hustle and bustle of busy DC streets, the park was a mini getaway for those who worked in any of the multi-story buildings that surrounded it. Resembling a wagon wheel, the park featured a redbrick paved main hub with redbrick paved spokes jutting out to curved concrete seating areas. Patches of grass and decorative flower beds lay in between the spokes. Ten-foot-high conifers stood guard around the central hub while black, column-like lamp posts encircled the entire park.

Mercy Sands sat on a metal three-person bench, its backside butting up to the first of three circular walls that, from the air, would have looked like a snowman. Inside the brick enclosures was more grassy land and tall, leafy trees.

Straight ahead of her, looking down the center of the street that stopped at the park, she could see the dome of the United States Capitol Building. Behind her, on her five o'clock, she could just make out the top of the Jefferson Memorial. Beyond it, two hours from sunset, the sun was still shining in a clear blue sky.

With her legs crossed at the knee, Mercy sipped from her cardboard 'to go' cup while watching the activity around her. Most men were dressed in suits, or khakis and sport coats, while a majority of women wore heels with skirts or dresses; all were likely beginning their journey home from work. Still congested, the streets and sidewalks were gradually thinning out.

She checked her watch, glanced over her right shoulder, then faced forward again while taking another drink.

Five minutes passed.

Dressed in blue jeans, a white blouse, and a dark-red jacket, her clothing was soaking up the sun's eighty-degree rays. Twenty-five minutes ago, the warmth had felt good. But now her body was releasing some of that warmth via perspiration. She thought about shedding the jacket, but her blouse underneath was cut lower at the neckline, and just the notion of someone getting a peek at her scars forced her to keep it on.

After checking her watch again, she sighed then downed the rest of her coffee while spotting a shadow appear on the sidewalk on her eleven o'clock. It grew taller before she felt a nearby presence.

A second later, a figure crossed in front of her and sat down on her left, at the far end of the bench. Dressed in a black suit, white shirt, and blue tie, he crossed his legs at the knee, gazing directly at the Capitol Building.

"I was starting to think you weren't going to show," said Mercy while placing her empty cup on the bench between her and him.

"Got tied up with a few last-minute requests." Terrance Duval faced Mercy. "I've been trying to reach you. I would've thought I'd be the first person you'd contact once you were back on American soil."

Spying him out of the corner of her left eye, she nodded. "Been tied up myself."

He turned toward the Capitol. "Glad you made it back safely. Too bad about Agent Freeman."

Mercy clenched her fists then forced herself to relax. "Yeah, he didn't deserve to die like that."

A minute of silence went by.

"So, what did you want to see me about?" asked Duval.

"Haven't seen any large deposits made to my bank account yet. When can I expect that 250 grand you promised me?"

He cleared his throat. "There's been a snag in the transfer. You know, red tape? Once that's taken care of, you should see the money shortly thereafter."

Pursing her lips, "No," she slowly shook her head, "no, I don't think I'll see a penny of that money."

Duval eyed her. "Pardon?"

She met his gaze. "After everything we've been through, are you really going to sit there and *lie* to me?" She watched him don a confused frown, or at least pretend he was confused. "I know the money's not coming, Terry. Just like I know you never expected me to make it out of Honduras alive."

"I'm not sure I follow."

Mercy chuckled then turned her head to stare straight down the street. "You've obviously thought this through, planned out every detail, so that none of it would blow back on you."

He opened his mouth to say something, but she cut him off with a raised left palm. "How about I save you the trouble of feigning ignorance?" A beat. "The money's not coming, because you never authorized me, or *anyone* for that matter, to fly to Honduras and bring back Romero. The flight from Iowa was private, most likely chartered through several cutouts to keep your fingerprints off any records. Plus, there was never any *team* scheduled to arrive after Freeman and me were in-country. That was all smoke and mirrors to get me there, so Romero could capture me and do to me," Mercy threw up an arm, "whatever his twisted, perverted mind wanted to do to me. I'm guessing for revenge's sake for what happened in the Caribbean." She turned toward Duval. "And somehow he got to you, didn't he?"

Duval was silent.

"How much did he pay you, Terry, to betray me?"

More silence.

"At first, I didn't want to believe it was you. I think on some level I knew, but I just couldn't bring myself to think you'd stoop this low. For crying out loud," she raised her voice, "I've gone to hell and back for you."

Moments passed.

"And then there's Walt Freeman," she said. "You sent a good man to his death. But only *after* he fed you everything you needed to know about our nightclub operation, though, right? I told him not to tell you, but," she paused, "but that wasn't in him. No. He had orders to keep you informed of every move we made, and that's exactly what he did." Mercy leveled a finger at Duval. "And that's how Romero knew where I would be and what I would be wearing that night." She wagged her head at him. "Freeman didn't have a clue you were using him."

Duval said nothing.

"So, tell me," Mercy continued. "How was it *supposed* to go down? Were Romero's men going to kidnap me off the street, break into my hotel room and drag me away? Or maybe a drive-by shooting. How was he supposed to kill me?"

Duval filled his lungs, exhaled, then squinted down the street. "Agent Freeman was a good little soldier; young, energetic, willing to please his boss. I'm sorry he's dead. He'll be missed."

Mercy screwed up her face. "You make me sick."

Duval grinned while wagging a finger at her. "*Prodigal*, you're one of the smartest, most talented agents—scratch that—*people* I've ever known or worked with. You have an uncanny ability to complete whatever task you set your mind to. Doesn't matter what the mission throws at you, you use whatever's in your environment to get the job done and make it back home. I admire that in you."

"Save your phony praise for someone who cares."

"No," he shook his head, "no, it's not phony. I'm truly in awe of your many talents. And I'm truly sorry we must end our relationship on this sad note and these wild accusations."

"Accusations you have yet to deny," Mercy countered.

Duval put both feet on the pavement. "Since I assume you have no actual proof of your claims, outside of what a cartel leader is right now saying to ICE investigators, which," Duval raised his right shoulder, "is really the word of a drug lord versus the word of a respected, long-time employee of the Agency," he faced her while lifting his butt off the bench, "I'll be leaving now."

"That's the thing about evidence. Even the best of plans can be tripped up by the littlest of things."

Duval sat back down.

Mercy retrieved a cell phone from her jacket pocket. "After I had Romero in custody, I snagged his cell phone off a nightstand. It was an afterthought, really. I thought it might come in handy if I needed to make a phone call." She eyed the phone's blank screen. "Never knew how valuable it would become."

"Oh?" said Duval. "How so?"

She crossed her arms over her belly, the phone in her right hand, under her left elbow. "Well, once I realized you had sold me out, I stopped talking to the ICE investigators and called someone I knew at the Agency, a good friend. He convinced the investigators to cut me loose late last night." She held a shrug. "After all, I had committed no crime in the US. No one from Honduras was calling the State Department to report any wrongdoing. And ICE had a wanted man delivered to their doorstep, so..."

Duval swallowed, his eyes dipping to the phone she held before coming back to her. "Sounds like the report I read."

"Anyway, after I was told I was free to go, I asked my friend if he could crack the password on," she held up the phone, "Romero's cell." Mercy faced Duval. "There are a lot of talented people at ICE who can do such things." She waved him off. "Who am I kidding? You already know that."

Both people sat in silence for the next thirty seconds, Duval studying Mercy, Mercy glancing around at the people moving about.

Duval looked down and rubbed his palm, his fingertips sliding over damp skin. "And?"

A few moments later, she lolled her head his way. "And a certain number kept popping up on Romero's call list." She smiled for the first time since she had grinned at a little girl who had waved at her earlier. "It was a number I instantly recognized."

Duval's chest heaved while his features turned sour. "Means nothing. He could've dialed the wrong number. He could've been trying to reach whoever had the number before its current owner. Not much evidence, I'm afraid."

"Yes, but when you add that to what Romero is claiming, as well as the testimony of a highly respected former agent who is," Mercy recalled what Freeman had said to her — *'You're something of a,' Freeman paused, 'a mini legend at the agency. People still talk about you, what you did'* — "who some say," continued Mercy, "is a mini legend at the agency, well, then it's certainly enough to open an investigation. Wouldn't you agree? And who knows what investigators are going to uncover? Wire transfers, perhaps?"

Duval ogled the phone she held, glimpsed his surroundings, then went back to staring at the device.

She noticed him, read his intentions. "You insult me, Terry. Do you *really* think I'd bring Romero's phone *with* me?" She dropped the mobile, her own mobile, into her jacket pocket and stood. Looking down at him, she couldn't help but feel some pity for the man. Being ambitious is a good thing; however, like most things in life, too much of a good thing can lead a person down the road to hell. From her heart, Mercy said to him, "May God forgive you of your sins," before she donned black sunglasses and walked away.

ONE MONTH LATER

The temperatures were close to ninety, but the air was dry. Thick and white fluffy clouds rolled across the sky, giving spectators and ball players relief from the blazing sun.

Sitting with her legs crossed at the knee, dressed in a white tank-top, a red skort, and a simple pair of white tennis shoes, Mercy adjusted her wide-brimmed straw hat, which was perfect for keeping the sun's rays from burning the back of her neck. And if she were being completely honest, the fashion accessory was also perfect for hiding things you didn't want people to see.

She glanced around. The players were finishing their warmups while nervous and excited parents sat elbow-to-elbow in the bleachers for the championship game. Seeing all those people jam-packed into a small space only reinforced the decision she had made to open a lawn chair down the right-field line, not too far from first base. Plus, she wasn't in a talking mood, hadn't been since getting back from Honduras. In fact, she took every chance she could to be by herself, to pray, to read the Bible, or to just simply close her eyes and listen.

In those quiet moments, she learned that being

betrayed, even by someone you weren't that close to, was a tough experience to move past. She understood forgiveness was key, but knowing and doing were sometimes worlds apart from each other, even for a woman who knew her own sins had been forgiven.

Mercy heard a ping. She grabbed her cell phone and read the incoming text message: *Check out the news.* The text was from her friend at ICE, the one who had helped secure her release after she had landed the Cessna Caravan in Florida a month ago.

She opened a browser and went to a couple news outlets. All of them were running a similar 'Breaking News' story. Tapping her phone's screen, a video began playing, a video of a male news anchor in a jacket and tie and a female anchor in business attire, sitting at a desk. Mercy pressed the 'volume-up' button a few times.

Man's voice: "...begin this hour with a late-breaking story coming out of the nation's capital."

Woman's voice: "That's right, Steve. Officials have announced the indictment of a current Immigration and Customs Enforcement agent."

Steve: "Fifty-eight-year-old Agent Terrance Duval has been charged with multiple crimes, including conspiring with the known leader of a drug and human trafficking cartel operating out of the Caribbean."

Diane: "Details are still coming in, but stay tuned to the 24/7 newsroom for continuing updates on this—"

Mercy stopped the video and slipped her phone into

the purse hanging from her chair. Initially, her heart had skipped a beat at the news. Justice was being served. Now, however, she put a hand to her stomach, hoping to ease her sudden nausea, ease the remorse welling up inside her. She had succumbed to the human condition's base instincts for taking pleasure in an enemy's misfortunes. After saying a prayer, asking for forgiveness, she settled into her chair, hoping the guilt would pass, and she could enjoy the game.

A minute later, Dacia came running up to Mercy, a baseball glove covering her left hand. She pointed back toward a girl her age. "Esta chica que conocí quiere que juegue a la pelota con ella. ¿Está bien, Mercy?"

Spying the girl Dacia had pointed at—the girl was lobbing a softball into the air and catching it—Mercy recognized her as the older sister of one of the boys on the team. She came back to Dacia and regarded her. Their relationship was still being fleshed out. Was Mercy a mother figure to the fifteen-year-old, a friend, or simply the woman who had killed to save an innocent teen from being further exploited? Smiling, happy the girl had the decency to ask instead of just going off on her own, Mercy nodded. "Seguro. Sí. Divertirse."

Dacia ran off while holding her glove in the air, the universal sign for 'toss me the ball.'

Mercy watched the girls throw the ball back and forth, marveling at how shared activities could bridge language barriers.

A man's voice: "She's got a strong arm."

Mercy looked toward home plate to see a man in blue jeans, brown hiking boot type shoes, and a dark-brown t-shirt, holding a lawn chair in one hand and a large cooler in the other. Her attention was drawn to the yellowish-gold shield emblazoned on the front of the t-shirt. Inside the shield, 'IOWA STATE PATROL' was printed in dark letters. She met his gaze. "Excuse me?"

He motioned toward the girls, specifically toward Dacia. "Your daughter has a strong arm."

Mercy glimpsed Dacia then shook her head. "No. She's not my daughter. She's from," Mercy paused, "from out of town, staying with me until I," she recalled all the work she had done to get the asylum process going for Dacia to remain in the United States, "until I can get a few things sorted out."

"I guess I shouldn't have assumed she was your daughter. My apologies."

"That's all right. No harm done."

He bent over and set the cooler down.

Mercy spotted a silver cross and silver chain pop out from under his shirt.

He opened his lawn chair a few feet away from her. "Is it okay if I sit here? I'm not in your way, am I?"

"No."

He stood taller. "No, I'm not in your way? Or, no, I can't sit here?"

Having heard how abrupt her response had been, she

softened her tone. "I mean, *no*, you're not in my way, and of course you can sit there. Free country, right?" she added with a smile.

He jerked his head to the side. "For *now*, anyway."

She bobbed her eyebrows. "Well, hopefully, it'll always be free."

"Amen to that," he said before sitting down on her eleven o'clock, his back to her.

Tilting her head at his reply, Mercy took in his broad shoulders, wide neck, and wavy hair, particularly the dark, 'S' shaped locks at the back. Her eyes went lower, to his 'big-as-a-python' upper arms stretching the limits of his t-shirt.

He glanced at her over his shoulder.

She turned away. A tick later, she eyed the back of his head again. "I'm sorry, but I haven't seen you at any of the games. Are you related to someone playing?"

He pointed. "My son's on first base. Robbie?"

"Really? So," Mercy frowned while scanning the bleachers, her mind's eye looking for the woman who had always brought Robbie to the games, "so, *JoAnn's* your wife then?"

"No." He faced her. "JoAnn is my sister-in-law. With me working second shift, I haven't been able to make any of the games."

Still frowning a bit, Mercy nodded a few times, her brain trying to connect the dots. She didn't know if he had noticed her 'wheels' spinning, but he ended up adding some clarification.

"My wife passed away two years ago," he said. "Breast cancer."

"Oh. I'm so sorry for your loss," said Mercy. "But I rejoice for your wife. She's in the arms of her Savior now. No pain, only joy."

His eyes lighting up, he squared shoulders with her and said, "Thank you. Thank you for that. Everybody always focuses on the survivor's pain, forgetting that the departed one is in a much better place. And *that* is cause for celebration."

"I agree." Mercy thought for a moment. "Looking back on it now, everybody kind of did the same thing to me when my husband passed."

"How long ago was that?"

"Eight years, before our son was born."

He grimaced. "I'm sorry to hear that. But I too rejoice," he paused, "for *your* spouse."

She smiled. "Thank you."

Time passed while the two simply stared at their offspring tossing baseballs around on the field, each one lost in his and her own memories.

"JoAnn's been a great influence on Robbie, but," the man shook his head once, "a kid needs both a father *and* a mother." He scratched his chin. "As a single parent, I do the best I can, trying to make up for what he's missing from his mom not being here, but sometimes I ask myself," he chewed on his lower lip, "is my best..."

"Is it enough?" interjected Mercy.

"...enough?"

Sitting up straighter in her chair, feeling a bond forming with this stranger, Mercy met his gaze and nodded. "Yeah."

He rose from his chair and extended his right arm. "I'm Jack, by the way. Jack Dunham."

"Mercy. Sands," she added while leaning toward him.

He clasped her hand while motioning toward the field. "Is your son out there, too?"

She pointed toward the pitcher's mound. "He's pitching."

Pumping her hand, "Wait a minute," Jack eyed the mound then pivoted back toward her, his left index finger still aimed at her son. "*John* is your boy?"

She nodded, surprised he knew her son's name.

"Wow. My sister-in-law has shown me video clips of him pitching." He shook his head at Mercy. "He has a wicked fastball for someone his age."

Mercy beamed.

He glanced down at the grass. "If I'm not mistaken, he struck out nine batters last game, didn't he?"

"Ten, actually," replied Mercy, "but who's counting?"

Jack sniggered. "Apparently, mom is."

The two shared a laugh, neither one aware that they were still holding hands.

"Well, it's nice to meet you, Mercy. And might I add, you have a beautiful name."

"Why, thank you," she replied, unsure if her chest was getting hot because the temps were rising or because something else was happening.

Jack looked down. "I'm sorry. You probably want this back, don't you?" He let go of her hand.

Smiling, she bounced a shoulder. *No hurry.*

He returned to his chair, stopped, then pointed at his cooler. "Would you care for a drink? I've got plenty. Soft drinks. Water."

Mercy raised an eyebrow at the cooler. "What soft drinks do you have?"

He told her.

"I think I'll have a water."

Jack dug out a bottle of water, unscrewed the cap, and handed it to her. "Here you go."

She smiled. "Thank you."

He twisted the lid off a water bottle for himself then took a drink.

Mercy sipped. Swallowing, she dipped her forehead toward his shirt. "Are you a state trooper?"

He glanced at his shirt then came back to her. "Retired."

She cocked her head. "But you said you were working second shift."

"At the hospital. I'm an EMT there."

She arched her brows. "No kidding."

He sat down and contorted his large frame in the rickety chair to see her. "Yeah, I quickly discovered retirement wasn't my thing."

"Service is in your blood, huh?"

He snickered. "I guess you could say that." A beat. "What about you?" He pulled on the arm of the chair to keep from corkscrewing back to the left. "What do you do for a living?"

"I work at the diner off thirty-five." Mercy hesitated. She never wanted to talk about her previous occupation. Inevitably, questions would be asked, questions she preferred not to answer. She half closed an eye at Jack. He seemed different, though, down to earth. And he seemed to have faith in God. So, she went out on a limb. "Before that, I was an ICE agent."

"No way," said Jack, going to his right hip, his sudden weight transfer nearly tipping over the chair. He steadied the lawn furniture while shooting her an awkward glance.

"You know," Mercy took a drink of water then motioned toward the grass on her left, "it might be better, *safer*, if you parked that thing over here."

Smiling from ear to ear, he picked up his chair, placed it on her nine o'clock and sat down. "You're right." He regarded her for a few moments. "It's *much* better over here."

She grinned back at him then glanced away. With her heart beating faster, and her chest warming—and pretty sure the added 'heat' wasn't because of the weather— Mercy couldn't help but wonder what new beginnings

God had planned for her.

Thank you for purchasing and reading *Far From Mercy*. I hope you enjoyed this faith-based patriotic action thriller. Now keep reading for a sneak peek at *BIG SKY*, the first book in the Wade Lockhart series. Set in Montana, *BIG SKY* is a modern-day crime thriller featuring a no-nonsense sheriff, beautiful scenery, and fast-paced action.

That's all for now. I'll be back soon with a new novel. Until then...

Blessings and Peace,

Alex

P.S. Don't forget your FREE ebook, *Escape & Evade*, at my website (AlexAnderNovelist.com).

Excerpt from BIG SKY

BIG SKY

MODERN SHERIFF CRIME THRILLER

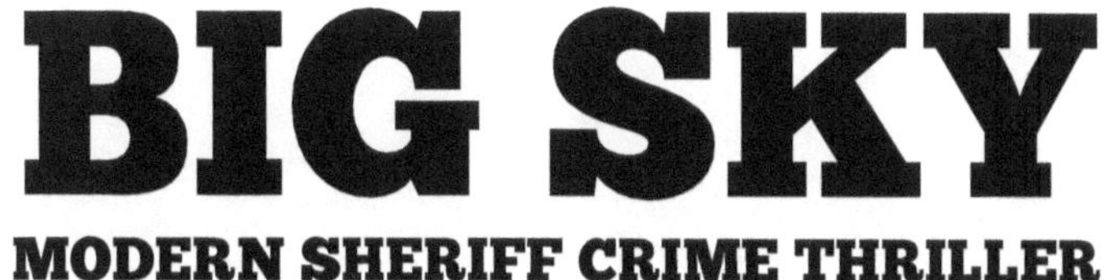

ALEX ANDER

Excerpt from BIG SKY

10 OCTOBER—8:57 A.M.
BIG SKY COUNTY
DUNBAR, MONTANA

Sporting wide, wood-grained panels on its sides and tailgate, a boxy, old-style, hunter green Jeep Grand Wagoneer stopped in the parking lot of a roadside motel, ten feet from the rear bumper of a newer Ford Explorer.

The dark brown—almost black—Explorer sat with its rooftop lights flashing, engine off. On the vehicle's front doors was a six-pointed star inside a circle. Centered on the star was Montana's state seal, with 'SHERIFF' above and 'SINCE 1895' below. The circle had 'BIG SKY COUNTY' above and 'MONTANA' below. Two olive branches, one adorning the right and left side of the circle, completed the logo for the sheriff's office. On the Ford's quarter panels, 'PROTECT & SERVE' was emblazoned. Both the logo and the letters were painted in a tannish-gold color.

The driver's door on the Jeep swung open.

Sliding off the Grand Wagoneer's sand-colored leather seats and entering fifty-degree temps on this calm morning, Sheriff Wade Lockhart got out of the vehicle, shut the door, and donned his black Resistol fur felt,

ALEX ANDER   153

cattleman-crown cowboy hat. The hat was trimmed with a silver-buckled black leather hat band, the buckle on the hat's left side. He tugged on the four-and-a-quarter-inch brim then eyeballed the motel.

Nearly a half a century old, the motel's painted brick façade was chipped and faded. What was once most likely white was now looking gray to black. Many of the metal room doors had patches of rust that had been painted over. But the rust was slowly reclaiming its dominance. On the second level, round metal handrails showed the same struggle between the elements and man's efforts to beat back nature.

Standing in the L-shaped motel's corner, a quarter mile south of town, near an old oil refinery, a web of 'fault lines' spanning the potholed parking lot ahead of his black Ariat pull-on work boots, Lockhart tipped his head back to spy a blue sky dotted with fluffy white clouds. His eyes took him toward the road, his attention settling on the mountains seven miles away.

Even though the clouds were patchy overhead, they were darkening and growing thicker above the mountain and beyond. Twelve hours from now, the upper elevations would get their first snowfall of the season while the residents of Big Sky would get rained on.

Located in southwest Montana, near the Rocky Mountain Front, Big Sky County ranked in the top five, in size, among all of Montana's counties. But it didn't even make the top ten in population.

          Excerpt from BIG SKY

Dominated by cattle ranches, Big Sky was made up of wide valleys of grasslands and sagebrush, and wooded riparian terrain that gave way to mountains, some of those peaks exceeding 10,000 feet in elevation.

The county, which on a map resembled an empty pop can with one side slightly dented, was also known to have some of the best trout rivers in the country. And when it came to big game hunting in Montana, nothing compared to Big Sky County. In fact, residents could boast that, every year, almost half of the state's elk harvest took place within its borders.

Demographically, Big Sky had a diverse mix of people—from sunup-to-sundown ranchers to miners, creatives, outdoor enthusiasts, entrepreneurs, and many more. Yet even with all their differences, residents could agree on one thing: everyone here enjoyed the simple things in life. Yes, if Montana symbolized a slow-paced, easy-going lifestyle, then Big Sky County was its flagship. Except on days like today.

Wearing blue jeans and a long-sleeved blue denim button-up shirt, Lockhart made his way toward the Ford Explorer's front bumper, toward a man conversing with a woman in her late twenties or early thirties.

At six-one, and one-sixty, the 45-year-old sheriff was a few pounds under his ideal bodyweight, his long legs and long arms adding to his spindly physique. The weight he carried, however, was all muscle. With a straight spine and a flat stomach, he walked 'tall,' projecting a confident demeanor that commanded people's attention, a surviving trait from the former Lieutenant Colonel's twenty years of service in the US Army.

Lockhart's hair was light brown, cut short, and had no grays. But his beard was another story. A dozen years ago, his facial hair had started graying. Today, if he let it grow for a week, he went from looking like a distinguished middle-aged man to an elderly gentleman in his mid-sixties. And his sky-blue eyes, and naturally long eyelashes—eyelashes any woman would kill for— couldn't save him if things got busy, and he didn't have time to shave.

"Thank you for your assistance, Miss," said a man dressed in a dark brown button-up shirt, blue jeans, brown cowboy boots, and a brown cowboy hat, much like Lockhart's hat. A black tie, held in place by a gold bar, accompanied a badge on the deputy's short-sleeved shirt. On his belt was a Glock 19 pistol and individual pouches for spare magazines, handcuffs, and a flashlight.

The young woman walked away, and the man at the front bumper dipped his chin at Lockhart. "Morning, Sheriff."

"Jace."

Jace scribbled onto a notepad then stuffed the pad and pen into his shirt's left breast pocket, his curled right arm showing off a bulging bicep. Proud of his physique, he always waited as long as possible before giving in to the colder temperatures and donning a jacket.

     Excerpt from BIG SKY

Lockhart eyeballed the 24-year-old man. Three inches taller, and much wider, and much stronger than Lockhart ever was, the young deputy could have easily been mistaken for a linebacker. And the man's blue eyes, light brown hair, chiseled jaw, and thousand-watt smile would have captivated the heart of every young lady within a mile radius.

Jace glanced beyond Lockhart's shoulder before poking his chin at the Jeep. "I see you decided to take the old girl out for a spin, huh?" He shook his head. "Can't believe that relic's still running. What is it...thirty years old now?"

"That's the trouble with kids these days," replied Lockhart. "You don't appreciate the classics, the finer things of life."

Jace chuckled. "Yeah, well," he tapped the hood of the Explorer, "this is just fine for me," a beat, "and with twice the horsepower of your dinosaur there."

"Careful. When I'm gone," Lockhart lifted a finger at the man, "I just might *will* you that dinosaur."

"Thanks, but *no* thanks."

The sheriff shot a glance toward the motel manager's office then faced the room nestled in the L-shaped structure's corner, the room's door wide open. "What do we have here, Deputy?"

"The assistant manager was doing her rounds this morning and came across an unconscious woman with a head wound in," Jace gestured behind him, toward the open room door, "that motel room. The assistant manager then called emergency services, who showed up and took the unconscious woman to the hospital."

"Do we have a name?"

"Candace Merriweather. She had no wallet, no purse, no ID on her."

"How'd we identify her so fast, then?"

"For whatever reason," Jace motioned toward the motel manager's office, "the assistant manager took a photo of Ms. Merriweather with her cell phone."

"You mean when the victim checked in?"

Jace shook his head. "After she called emergency services."

Lockhart scowled at his deputy.

The younger man shrugged. "Likes, happy faces on social media," a beat, "I don't know. But if it weren't for that photo, we wouldn't have gotten the victim's name so soon, so," he let his words hang in the air.

"How is Ms. Merriweather doing? Do we know?"

"I called the hospital, and they say she's in critical condition and still unconscious. Apparently, she has considerable brain swelling."

Lockhart made a face. "What else do we know about Ms. Merriweather?"

"She works over at The Bronc," replied Jace.

The Buckin Bronco, locally known as 'The Bronc,' was a mega complex of entertainment in Buck, Montana. The complex included a fancy, multi-floor hotel, poker

          Excerpt from BIG SKY

and slots gambling room, pool hall, high-end strip club, restaurant, lounge bar, and horse racing track. Located not too far from where Lockhart and Jace were right now, The Buckin Bronco sat close to an interchange, so it brought in patrons from across the state as well as travelers passing through the state.

"Doing what?" asked Lockhart.

"Dancing. Piper's there now." Piper was another of Lockhart's deputies. "She's getting more information on our vic from employees."

"What about when the victim checked in? Did the manager say anyone else was with her?"

"I don't know. The manager arrived right before you did. He's the one smoking over there. I was going to go talk to him after I finished up with," Jace gestured, "that woman I was speaking to when you drove up."

Lockhart nodded then glimpsed the smoking man over his shoulder. Sucking hard on the cigarette, the middle-aged man was dressed in dirty, ripped brown canvas pants, unlaced boots, and an open jacket over a muscle shirt, his hair tousled and greasy. Lockhart faced his deputy. "I'll question him. You still have things to do yet?"

"I've spoken to everyone who's renting a room right now, and I'm just about done processing the," he hooked a thumb over his shoulder, "the scene inside." Jace frowned. "It's weird, Sheriff. The motel room looks as if it's been scrubbed."

"Scrubbed?"

"Not professionally, I mean, like you'd see in the movies—guys in white suits with bleach. But everything in there is neat and tidy. Nothing's been knocked over or broken, like you'd expect to see if there had been some sort of struggle. And one more thing that's interesting." He pointed at a room two doors down from the scene. "I spoke with a man staying there, and he said he was awakened by the sound of vacuuming this morning."

"What time was that?"

"The witness said he thinks it was around five or five-thirty."

"What about the assistant manager? When did she get here?"

"See, that's what I thought, too," said Jace, "but her shift didn't start until seven."

Lockhart nodded while squinting at the motel rooms. *Unless they're a neat nick, who vacuums a motel room?* Two seconds passed. "All right. Good work, Deputy. When you're done, get back to the office and type up your report."

"Yes, sir. One last thing, Sheriff. That woman I was speaking to when you pulled up told me she saw two men near the scene early this morning."

"Did she describe them?" asked Lockhart.

"It was still dark, but she could make out that one had on a red-checkered flannel shirt. The other was wearing a long coat and had a cowboy hat on."

     Excerpt from BIG SKY

"What about skin color, height, weight?"

"The only thing she said was that both were taller than the truck they had gotten into...which was a dark-colored, older model with a missing tailgate."

Lockhart ran a knuckle over his chin. "What time was this?"

"The witness thinks she got up to go to the bathroom around six in the morning. That's when she looked outside and saw the men."

Vacuuming at five or five-thirty, then two men getting into a truck at six, mused the sheriff. "All right. If you get anything more on these guys, let me know."

"Yes, sir."

Lockhart marched toward the motel manager. He greeted the man with an extended right hand and a curt smile. "Sheriff Wade Lockhart."

"I know who you are," said the manager. "I seen all them posters around when you was running."

"And you are?"

"Lee Huntley."

The men shook hands.

"What can you tell me about what happened, Mr. Huntley?"

Huntley flicked ashes from his half-smoked cigarette. "What do you want to know?"

"Well, I'm sure you've seen the photo your," Lockhart motioned, "assistant manager took of the victim. Do you recognize her?"

"Nope. Never see—" Huntley hacked into his hand for a few seconds, "never seen her before."

"And yet she was staying in one of your rooms."

"Look," the manager sucked then blew out a cloud of smoke, "people of all sorts come here for all sorts of reasons. The biggest reason is to do stuff with people who they ain't supposed to be doing stuff with. I don't ask questions. I don't ask for names. And I only take cash." He shrugged. "As long as they don't destroy the room, I don't get involved in their goings-on."

"Who was on duty last night?"

"I was."

"Do you at least recall who rented the room she was found in?"

Huntley held a shrug. "Lots of people come through here. They all start to look alike."

"Did you hear any sounds last night...screams, shouts for help?"

The manager cocked his head at Lockhart while raising his brows. "Sheriff, I hear all kinds of screams and shouts and loud groans and moans all night long." A beat. "Early on, I made the mistake of investigating those sounds." The man shook his head. "I ain't no prude, but what I walked in on made the hair on the back of my neck stand up. You know what I'm saying?"

Lockhart leaned left to spy a camera mounted on the wall behind the office counter. He pointed. "I'm going to need the surveillance footage from that."

     Excerpt from BIG SKY

Huntley pivoted to see what the lawman was referring to. "Ha." He flicked his cigarette butt onto the pavement. "That's for show. Ain't hooked up to anything. It's only there to make robbers think twice."

A frustrated Lockhart plopped hands onto his hips and expelled a long breath. "Well, Mr. Huntley, you've been a huge help in this investigation." He did his best to keep his sarcasm in check. "The residents of Big Sky County thank you for your cooperation."

"Are we done here?"

"We're done here. But before I go," Lockhart leveled a finger at the butt the man had tossed, "I *am* going to need you to pick that up."

Huntley glimpsed his discarded cancer stick then eyed the sheriff. "This is private property."

Lockhart cited some outdated blight law that was still on the books, a law he had never enforced before, until now. "So, unless you want me to write you a citation, sir..."

Huntley rolled his eyes then stooped to snag the cigarette before standing tall and facing the sheriff.

Lockhart pinched the front brim of his hat and gave it a downward tug. "Much obliged, sir. You have yourself a good day now, you hear?"

Halfway to his Jeep, Lockhart felt his cell phone vibrate. He flipped open the tiny black device he used for phone calls only. Texting, and surfing the Internet, were not his thing. It wasn't as if he was averse to technology.

He had used it every day in the military. No. He simply chose to keep his screen time to a minimum. Plus, he preferred old-fashioned communication—talking to people. Ironically, though, if asked, most people would say he was a better listener than he was a talker. He put the mobile to his ear. "Lockhart."

In his ear, a young woman's voice: "Hey, Wade. It's Piper. I'm here at The Bronc. I'm questioning employees who work with the vic, Candace Merriweather, the one from the motel?"

"I know. Jace told me. What have you got?"

"I still have a couple more people to interview, but I wanted to get this to you. Two people chatted with the vic after her shift was over last night. Both said they think she left before seven-thirty. That tracks since her last act ended around seven. One of those who spoke with her said Candace mentioned *stopping by the bar* on her way home."

"Do we know which bar?"

"No, but she lives in Dunbar." Silence. "And there's one bar in that town that's right around the corner from where she lives. Employees say it's her go-to watering hole. In fact, you were just there not too long ago."

Lockhart nodded, his face becoming stoic. "Treadways?"

"Treadways," confirmed the deputy.

"All right. I'll check it out."

"Want me to back you up?" pressed Piper. "You're

          Excerpt from BIG SKY

not exactly their best customer there."

"No. I'll be fine. You finish what you're doing and then go to the hospital. Find out how the victim is doing and when they think she'll be awake. I want you to question her as soon as the doctors say it's safe to do so."

"Sure thing. Be careful, Wade."

"I will." Lockhart clicked off, stowed his mobile, then approached Jace near the Ford Explorer. "How much longer before you're done?"

"Fifteen minutes or so."

"I'll give you a hand and speed things up. We might have a new lead."

Excerpt from BIG SKY

9:31 A.M.

Treadway's Bar & Casino was located one block west of Main Street in Dunbar. The structure looked like three large metal storage buildings joined at different angles. With a flat roof, sides painted a dull gray, two exterior windows, and a gravel parking lot, its signage's paint peeling, Treadways would have been a perfect location for filming the next great zombie movie. Throw in a dozen or so slow-moving, rotting humanoid creatures among the five rusting cars and three pristine Harley-Davidsons parked near the building, yell 'action,' and let the cameras roll.

Lockhart parked his Grand Wagoneer in the parking lot just off the side street. At least he guessed he was off the street, since parking-lot gravel and road gravel had commingled.

Jace's Ford Explorer rolled to a stop on the Jeep's right.

Each man got out and opened his vehicle's tailgate.

Lockhart retrieved a Henry Repeating Arms Big Boy Steel Side Gate lever action rifle from a secured case bolted to the Jeep. A black sleeve held fourteen cartridges on the dark brown wooden buttstock's left side. Under the gun's rear peep sight, another sleeve wrapped around the underside of the forend and held nine more rounds. All totaled, the gun had thirty-four rounds stored in and on it, making it an 1890s version of a modern-day AR-15, albeit with a slower reloading rate.

Sliding the last three fingers of his left hand into the gun's loop, he lowered the lever just enough to verify a 44 Remington Magnum round was in the chamber, squeezed the action shut again, and closed the Jeep's tailgate.

Hunched over, under the Explorer's tailgate, Jace turned on the red dot scope on his Colt Law Enforcement M4 Carbine before readying the 5.56mm rifle and slinging it in front of his chest. He closed the tailgate and faced the sheriff. "Front door, back door?"

Holding his lever gun by the receiver, down by his right thigh, Lockhart nodded. "Give me thirty seconds before you make an appearance."

The deputy nodded.

"And Jace?" Lockhart scratched his chin, his features turning sour. "Watch yourself, son. I don't need anything happening to you."

"Will do, Sheriff."

The men strode toward the building, a rising sun throwing their shadows ahead of them, toward their ten o'clock.

Jace veered right and hurried along the right side of the bar.

     Excerpt from BIG SKY

Lockhart took a breath, exhaled, then opened the front door.

www.ingramcontent.com/pod-product-compliance
Lightning Source LLC
Chambersburg PA
CBHW061449150726
47987CB00001B/383